# allad o
# aYa

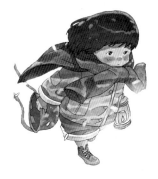

## Book 6: Lost

Written by
Jean-Marie **Omont**   Patrick **Marty**   Charlotte **Girard**

Illustrated by
Golo **Zhao**

Created and Edited by
Patrick **Marty**

Localization, Layout, and Editing by Mike Kennedy

**MAGNETIC**™

www.magnetic-press.com

YAYA AND TUDUO FOLLOWED THEIR HELPFUL NEW FRIEND CHAN TO THE SAFETY OF A NEARBY VILLAGE WHERE SHE HOPED TO FIND HER MISSING DAUGHTER. BUT TUDUO WAS STILL SICK WITH A FEVER AND NEEDED TO REST, SO CHAN GAVE HIM SOME PILLS TO HELP HIM SLEEP. SHE THEN TOOK YAYA WITH HER TO FIND HER LITTLE GIRL, BUT THINGS TURNED OUT TO BE MORE SINISTER THAN SHE THOUGHT! CHAN'S DAUGHTER WAS BEING HELD BY A STRANGER, AND CHAN WANTED TO TRADE YAYA FOR HER! YAYA WAS ABLE TO RUN AWAY AND ESCAPE BY JUMPING OFF A CLIFF INTO THE RIVER BELOW...

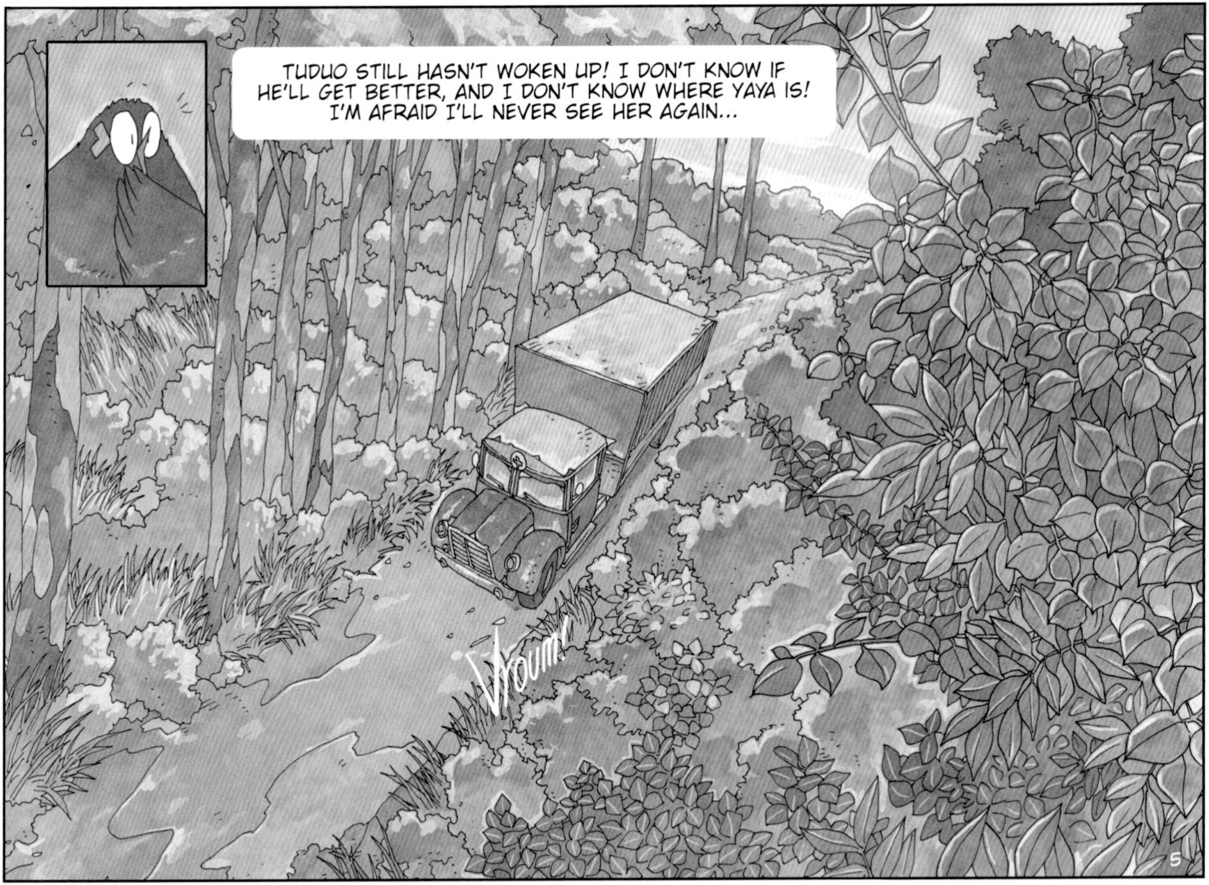
TUDUO STILL HASN'T WOKEN UP! I DON'T KNOW IF HE'LL GET BETTER, AND I DON'T KNOW WHERE YAYA IS! I'M AFRAID I'LL NEVER SEE HER AGAIN...
Vroum!

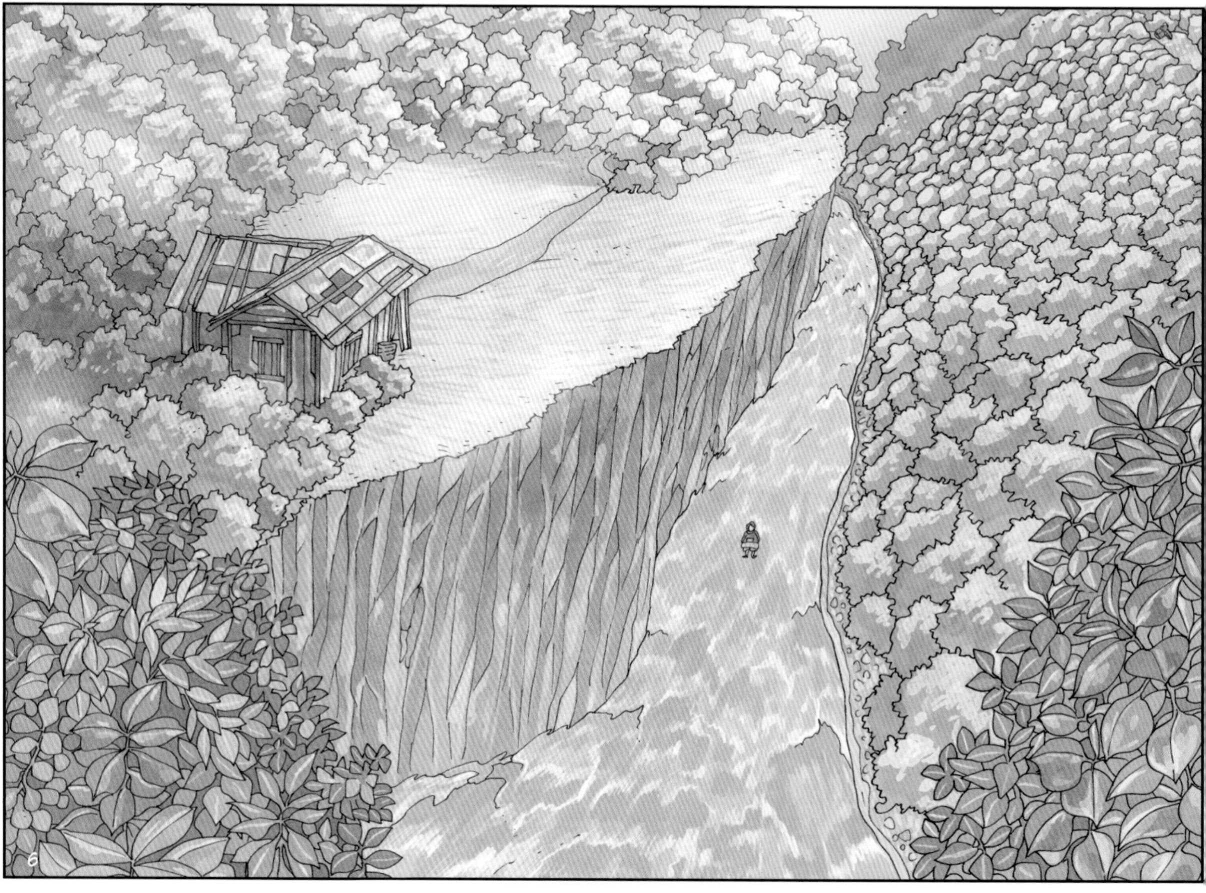

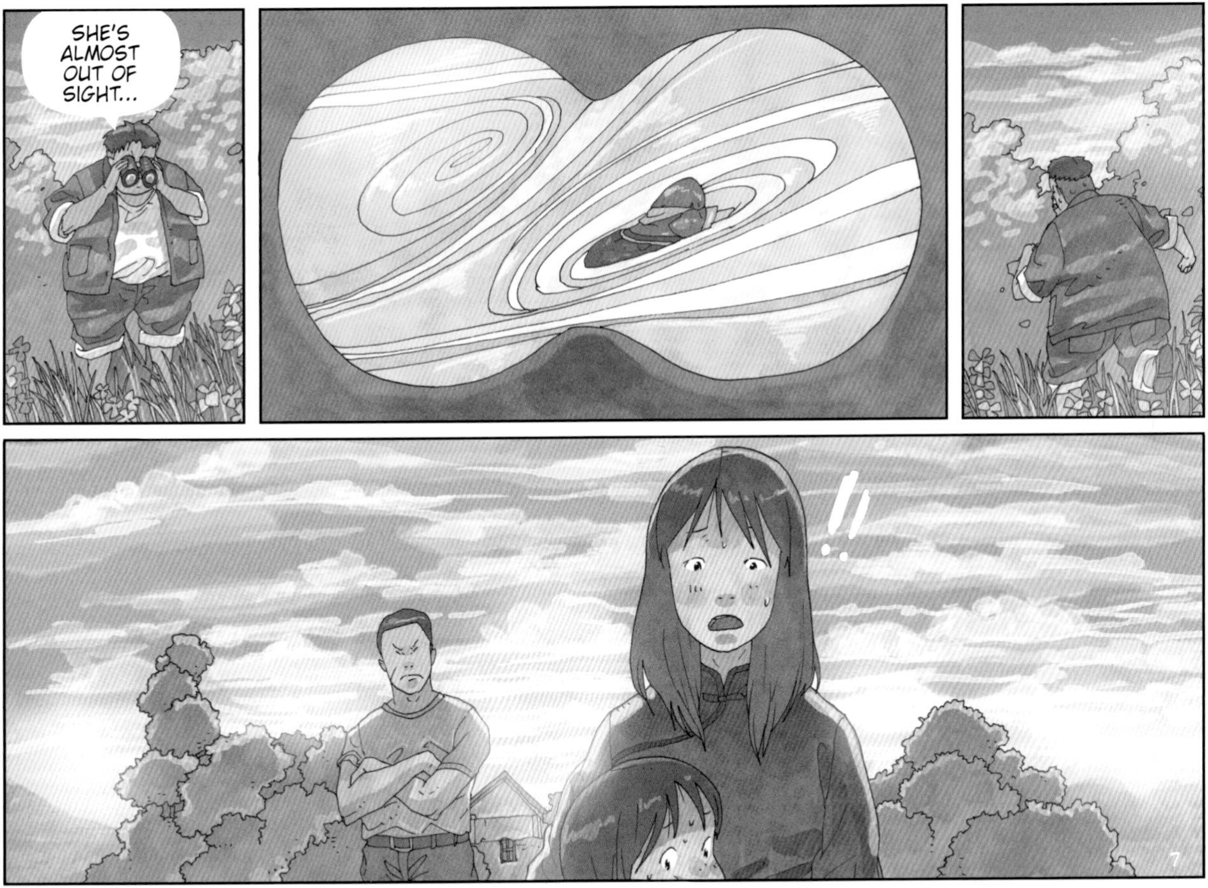
SHE'S ALMOST OUT OF SIGHT...
!!

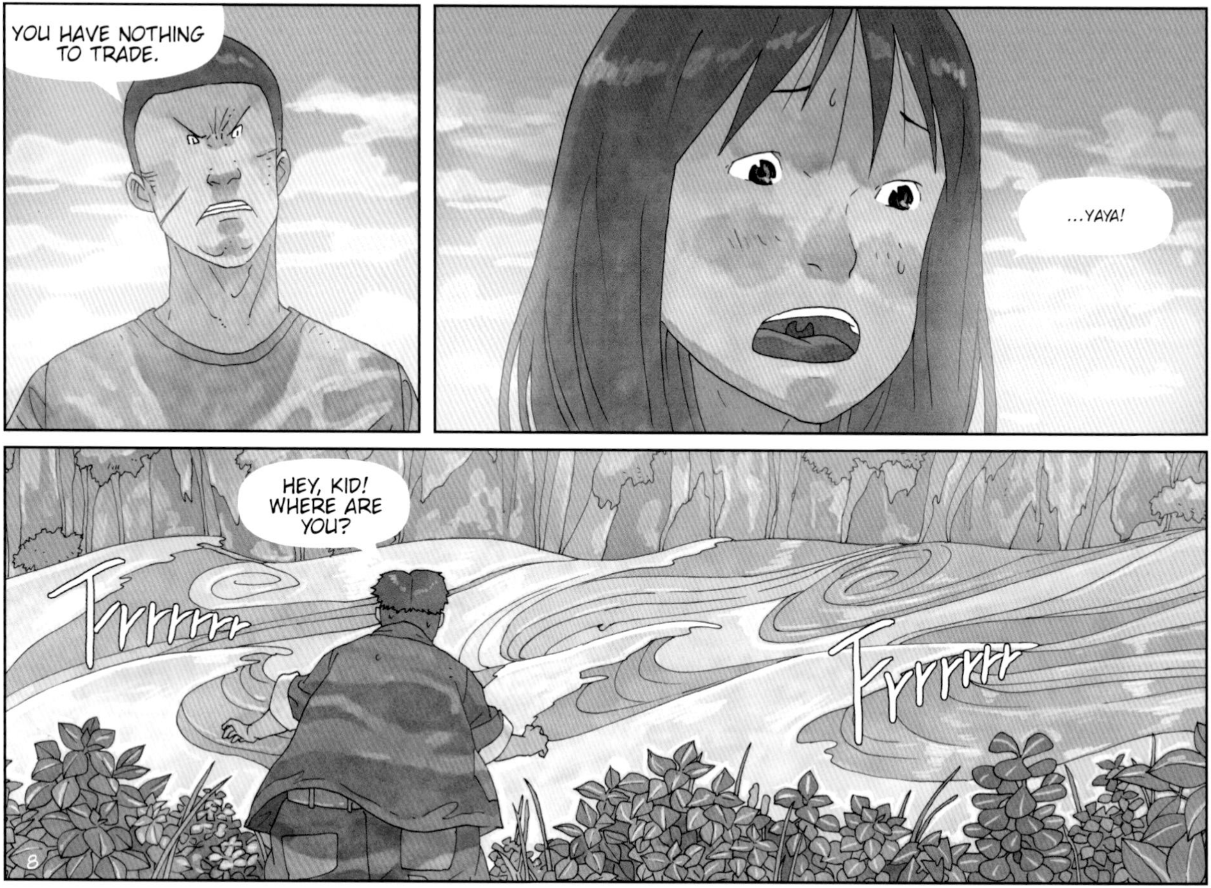
YOU HAVE NOTHING TO TRADE.
...YAYA!
HEY, KID! WHERE ARE YOU?
Frrrrrr
Frrrrr

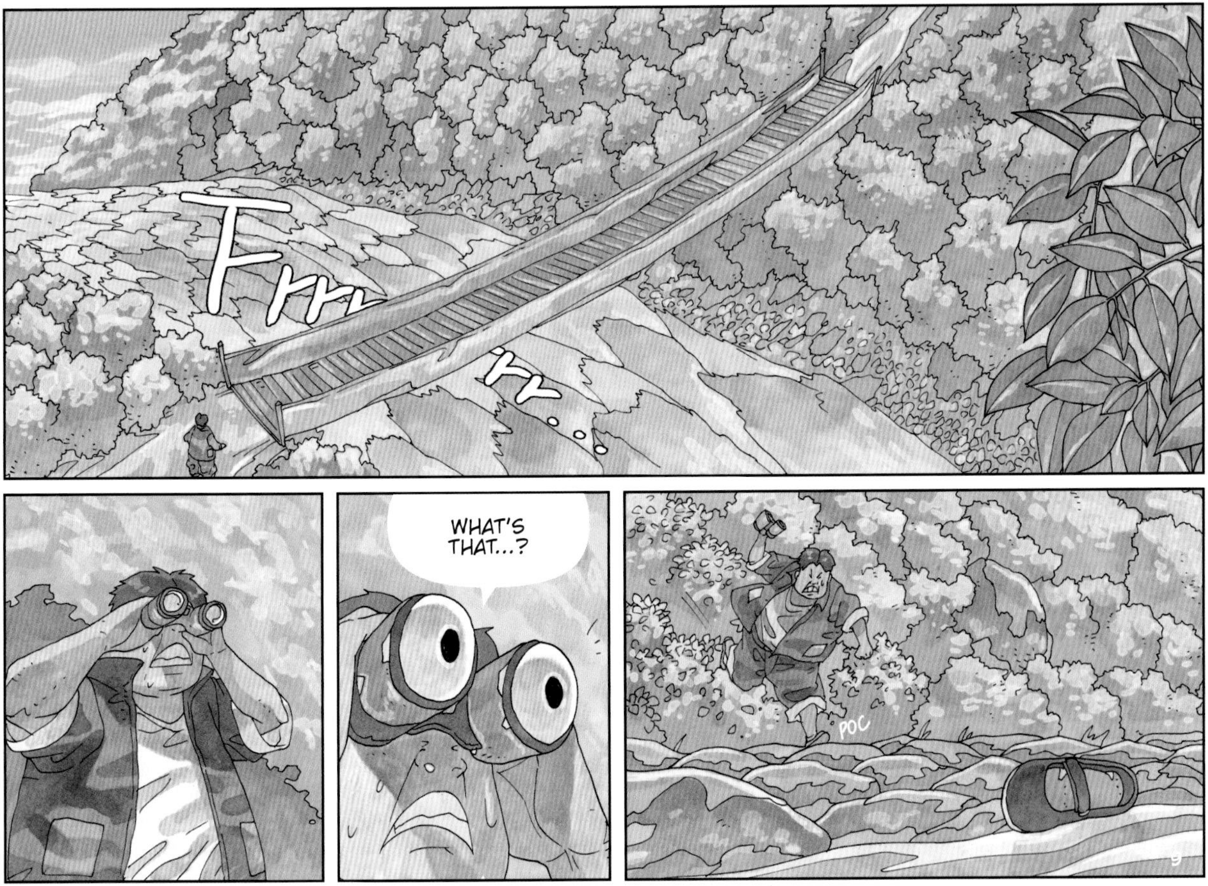
Frrrrrrr...
WHAT'S THAT...?
POC

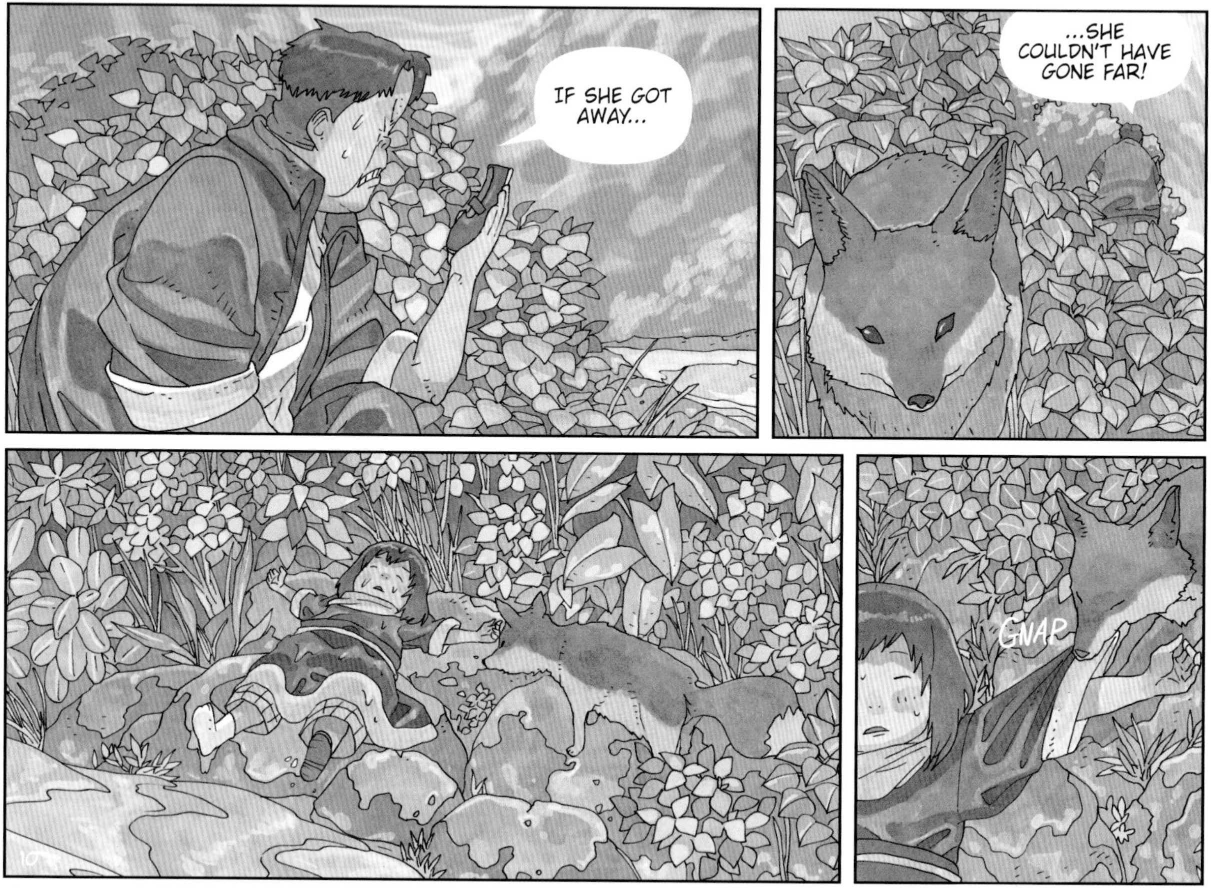
IF SHE GOT AWAY...
...SHE COULDN'T HAVE GONE FAR!
GNAP

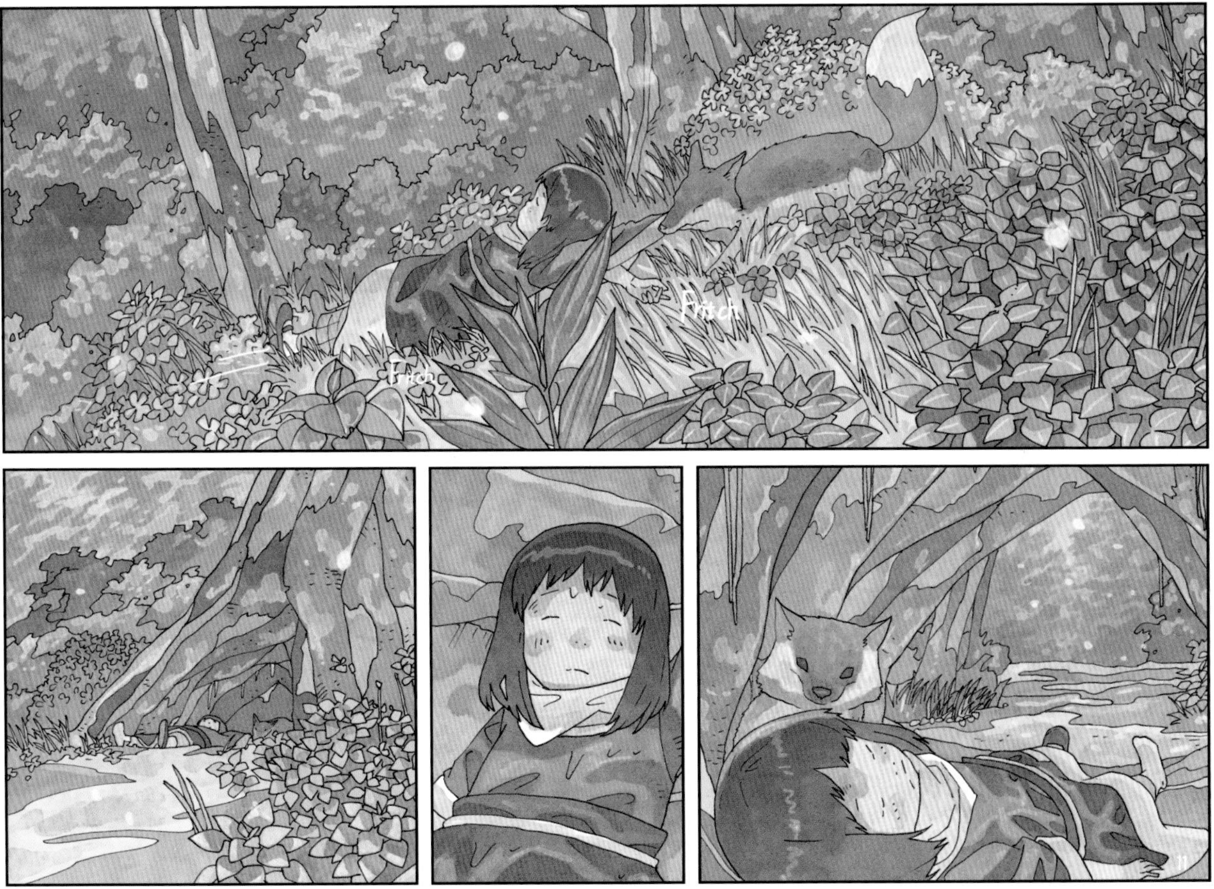
Fritch
Fritch

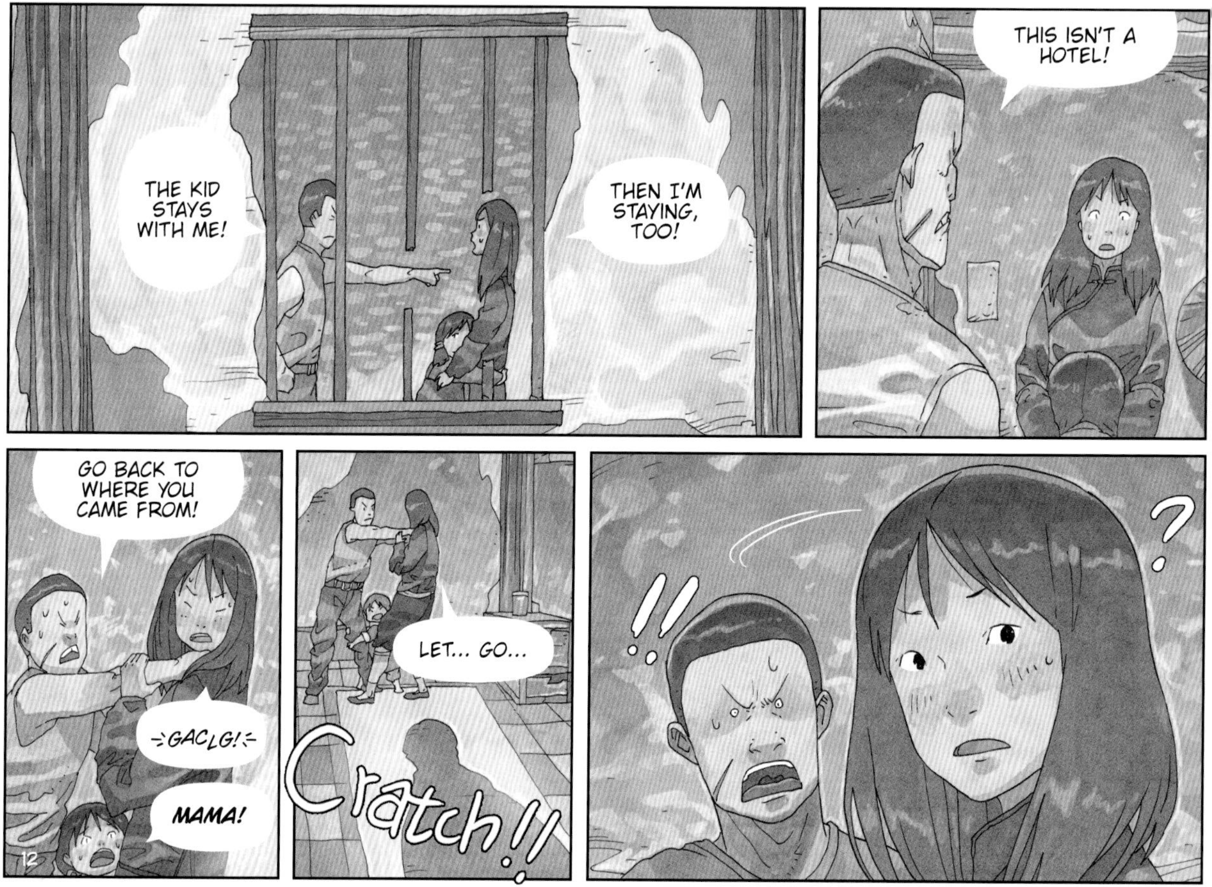
THE KID STAYS WITH ME!
THEN I'M STAYING, TOO!
THIS ISN'T A HOTEL!
GO BACK TO WHERE YOU CAME FROM!
GACLG!
MAMA!
LET... GO...
Cratch!!
!!
?

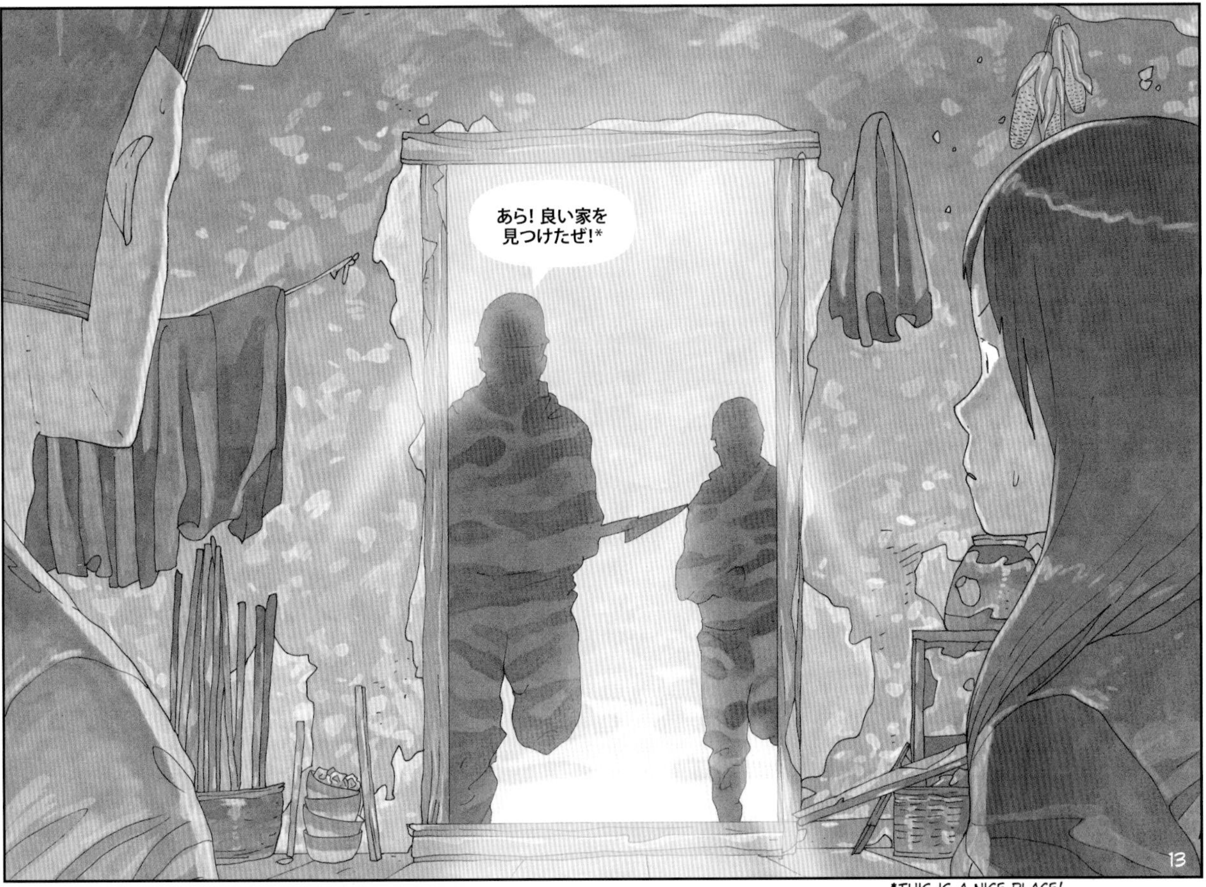

あら! 良い家を
見つけたぜ!*



*THIS IS A NICE PLACE!

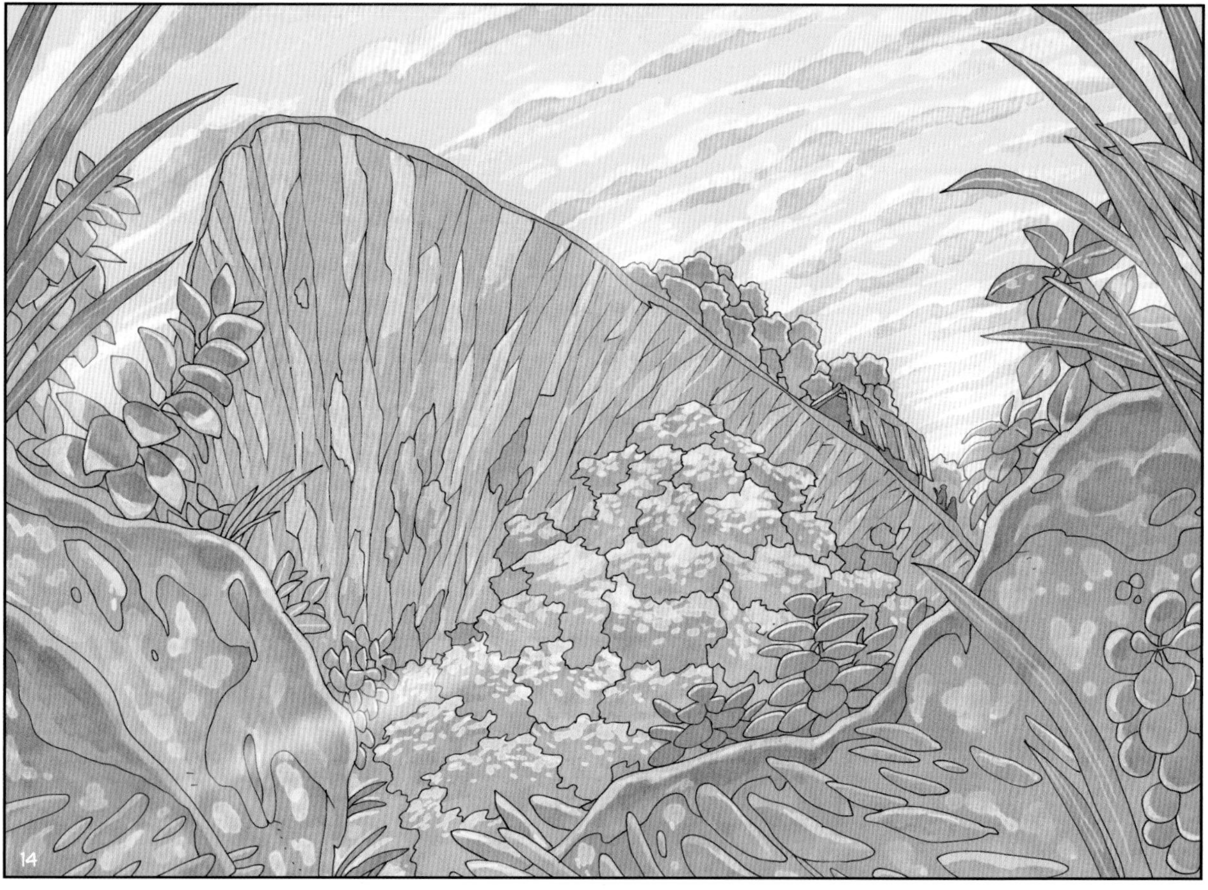

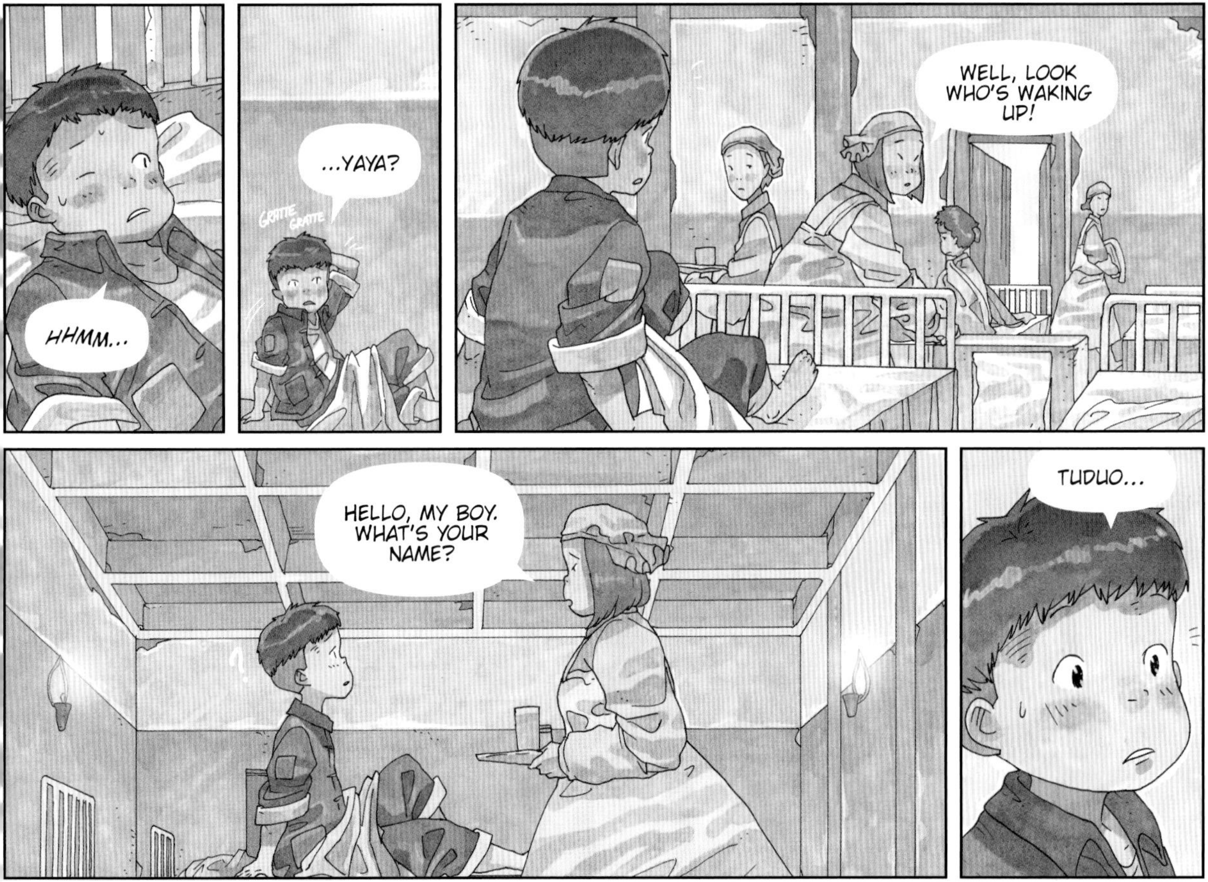
HHMM...
GRATTE GRATTE
...YAYA?
WELL, LOOK WHO'S WAKING UP!
HELLO, MY BOY. WHAT'S YOUR NAME?
TUDUO...

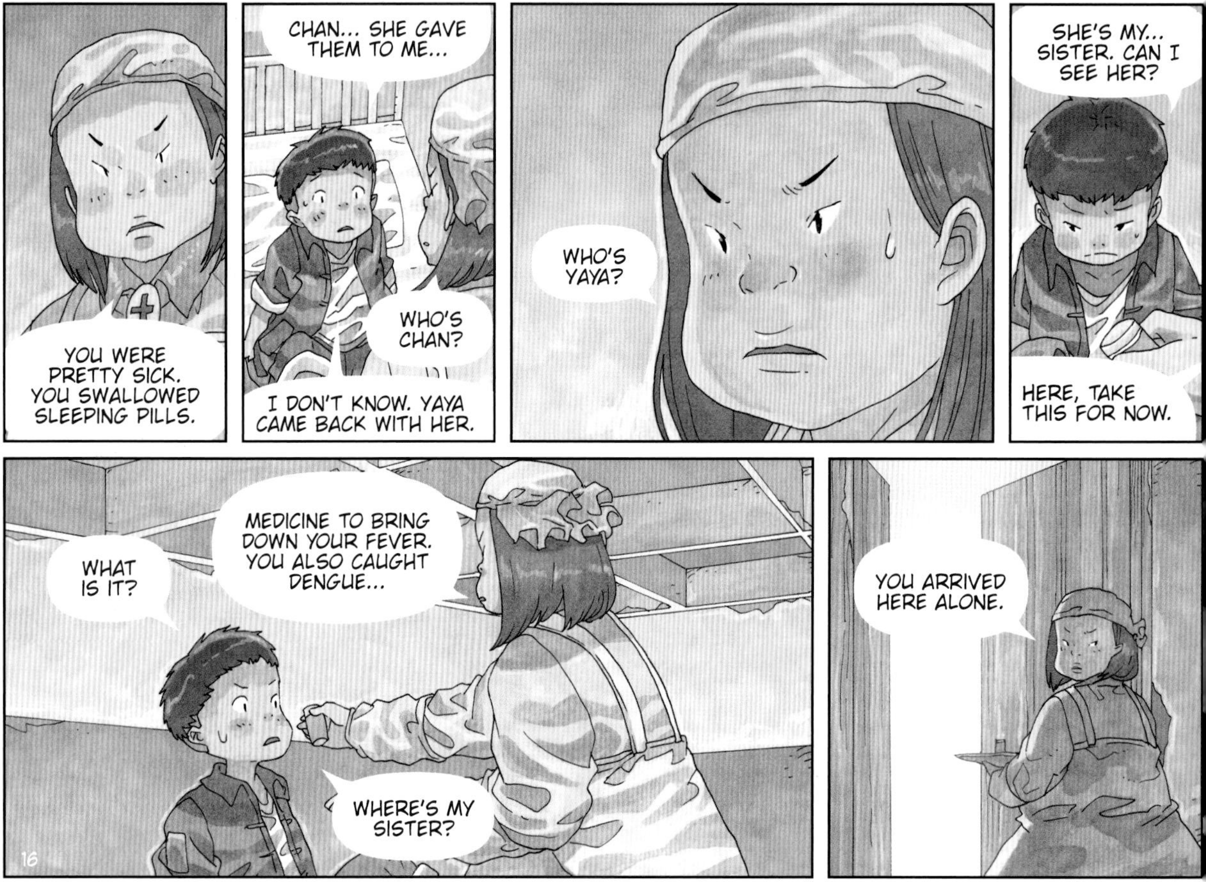
YOU WERE PRETTY SICK. YOU SWALLOWED SLEEPING PILLS.
CHAN... SHE GAVE THEM TO ME...
WHO'S CHAN?
I DON'T KNOW. YAYA CAME BACK WITH HER.
WHO'S YAYA?
SHE'S MY... SISTER. CAN I SEE HER?
HERE, TAKE THIS FOR NOW.
WHAT IS IT?
MEDICINE TO BRING DOWN YOUR FEVER. YOU ALSO CAUGHT DENGUE...
WHERE'S MY SISTER?
YOU ARRIVED HERE ALONE.

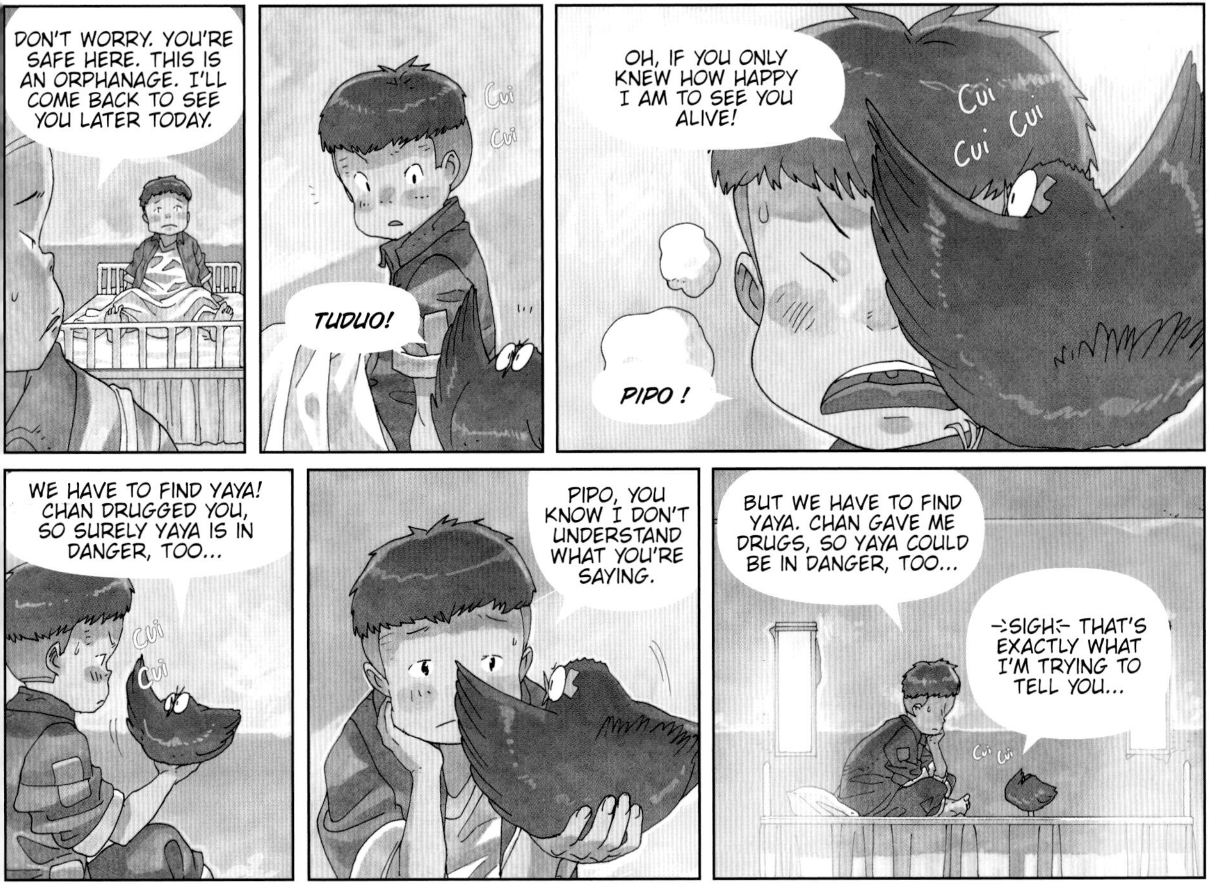
DON'T WORRY. YOU'RE SAFE HERE. THIS IS AN ORPHANAGE. I'LL COME BACK TO SEE YOU LATER TODAY.
Cui
Cui
TUDUO!
OH, IF YOU ONLY KNEW HOW HAPPY I AM TO SEE YOU ALIVE!
Cui
Cui Cui
PIPO !
WE HAVE TO FIND YAYA! CHAN DRUGGED YOU, SO SURELY YAYA IS IN DANGER, TOO...
Cui
Cui
PIPO, YOU KNOW I DON'T UNDERSTAND WHAT YOU'RE SAYING.
BUT WE HAVE TO FIND YAYA. CHAN GAVE ME DRUGS, SO YAYA COULD BE IN DANGER, TOO...
SIGH THAT'S EXACTLY WHAT I'M TRYING TO TELL YOU...
Cui Cui

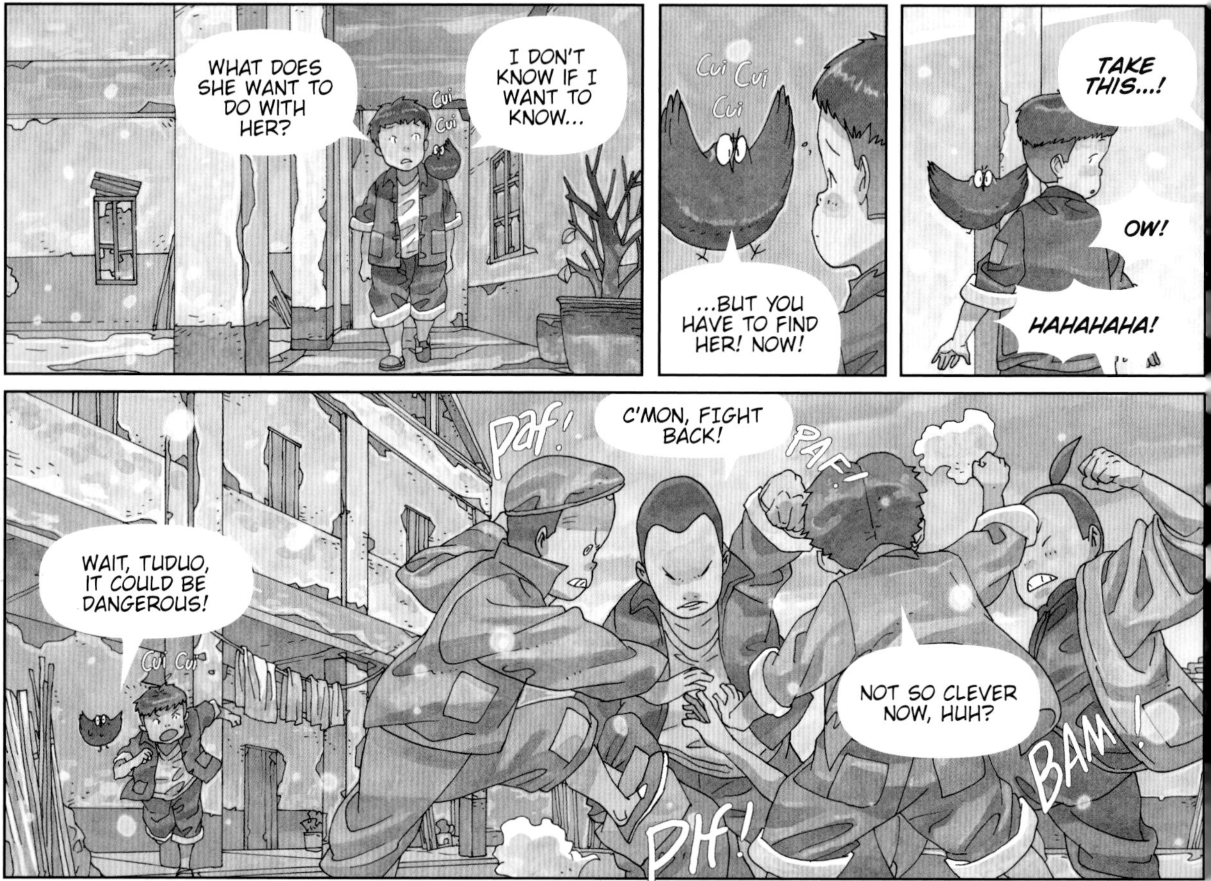
WHAT DOES SHE WANT TO DO WITH HER?
Cui
Cui
I DON'T KNOW IF I WANT TO KNOW...
Cui Cui
Cui
...BUT YOU HAVE TO FIND HER! NOW!
TAKE THIS...!
OW!
HAHAHAHA!
Paf!
C'MON, FIGHT BACK!
PAF!
WAIT, TUDUO, IT COULD BE DANGEROUS!
Cui Cui
NOT SO CLEVER NOW, HUH?
BAM!
Pff!

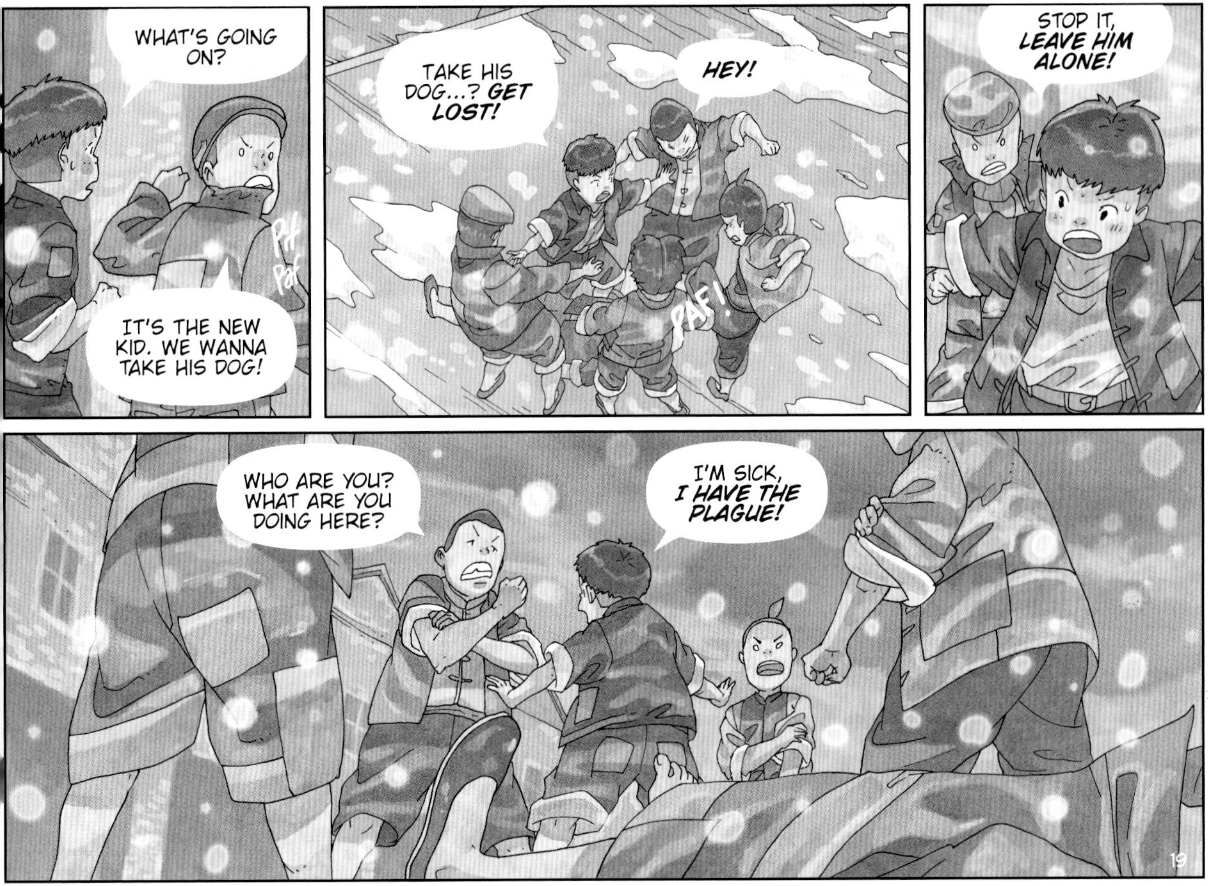
WHAT'S GOING ON?
IT'S THE NEW KID. WE WANNA TAKE HIS DOG!
Paf Paf
TAKE HIS DOG...? GET LOST!
HEY!
PAF!
STOP IT, LEAVE HIM ALONE!
WHO ARE YOU? WHAT ARE YOU DOING HERE?
I'M SICK, I HAVE THE PLAGUE!

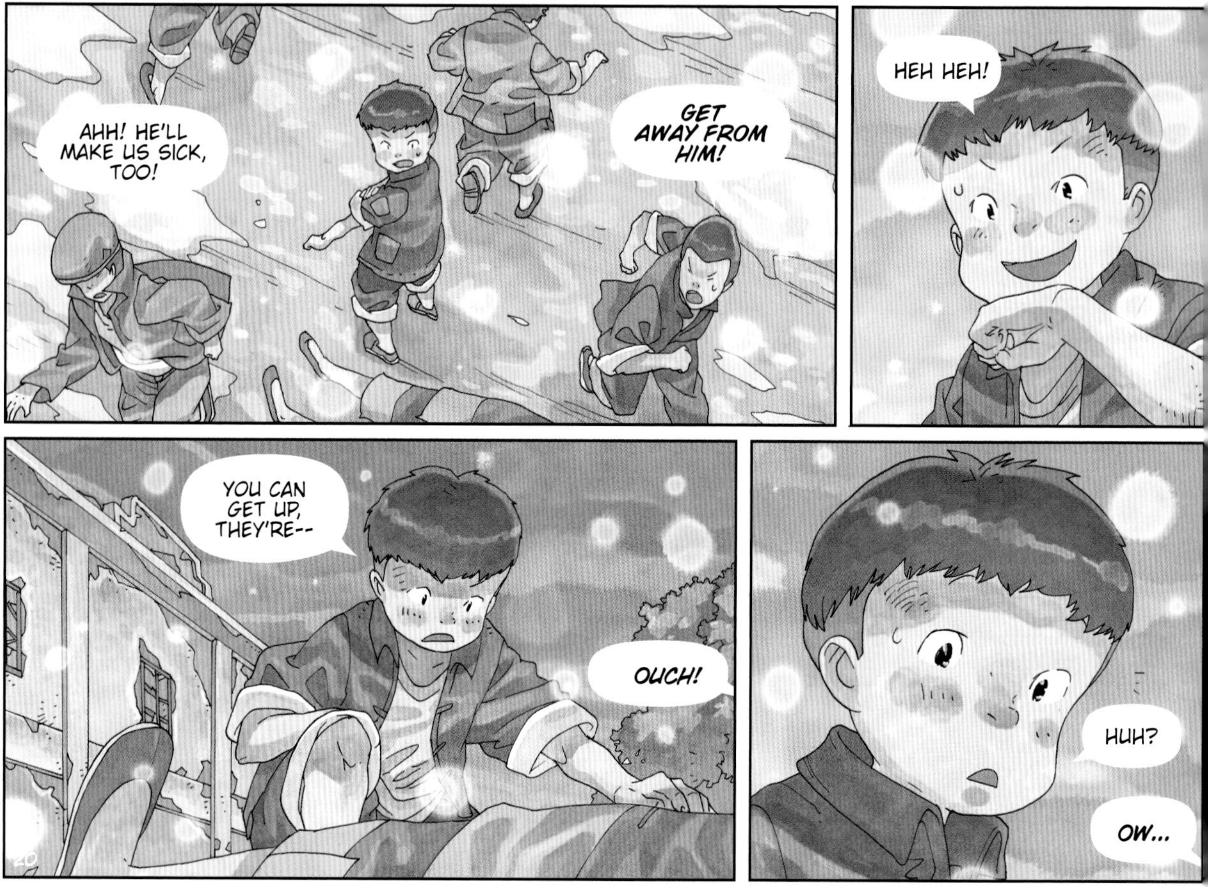
AHH! HE'LL MAKE US SICK, TOO!
GET AWAY FROM HIM!
HEH HEH!
YOU CAN GET UP, THEY'RE--
OUCH!
HUH?
OW...

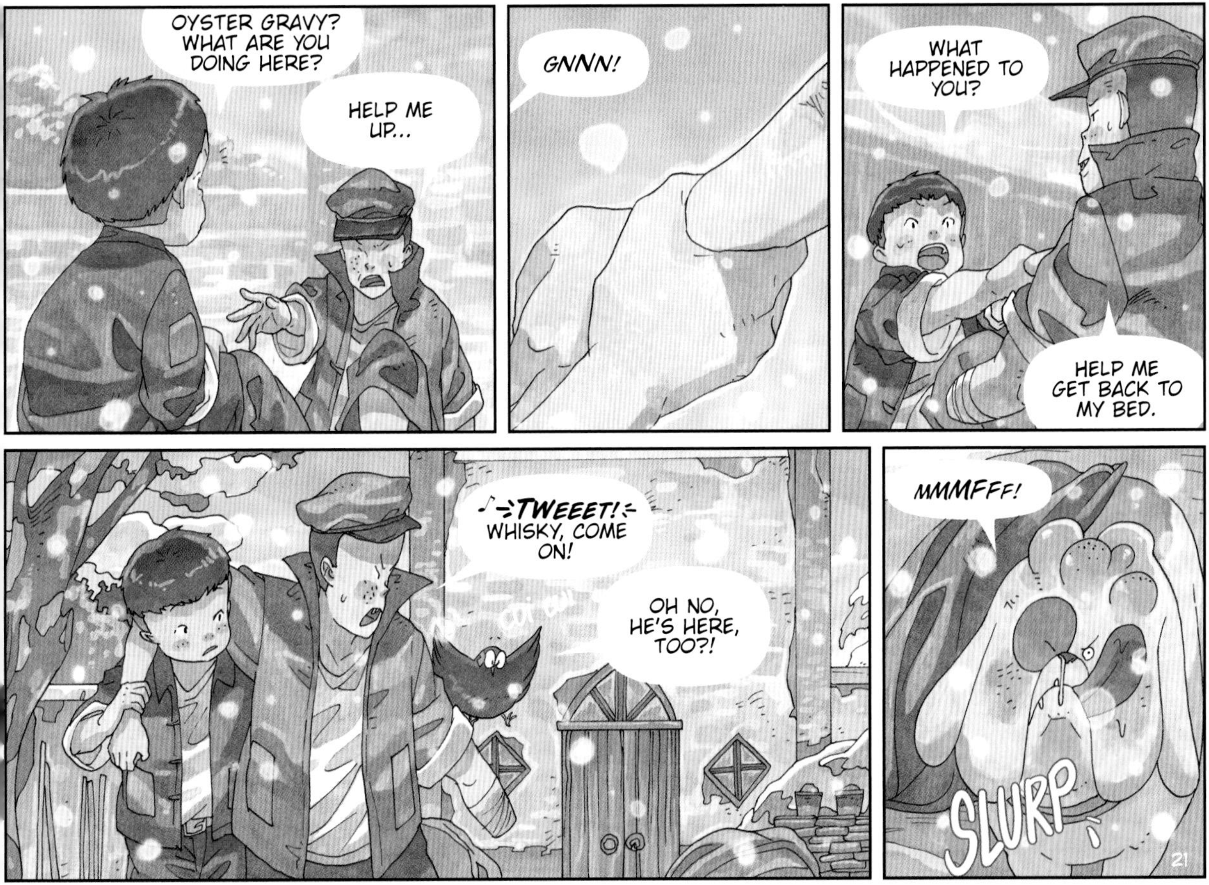
OYSTER GRAVY? WHAT ARE YOU DOING HERE?
HELP ME UP...
GNNN!
WHAT HAPPENED TO YOU?
HELP ME GET BACK TO MY BED.
TWEEET! WHISKY, COME ON!
OH NO, HE'S HERE, TOO?!
MMMFFF!
SLURP

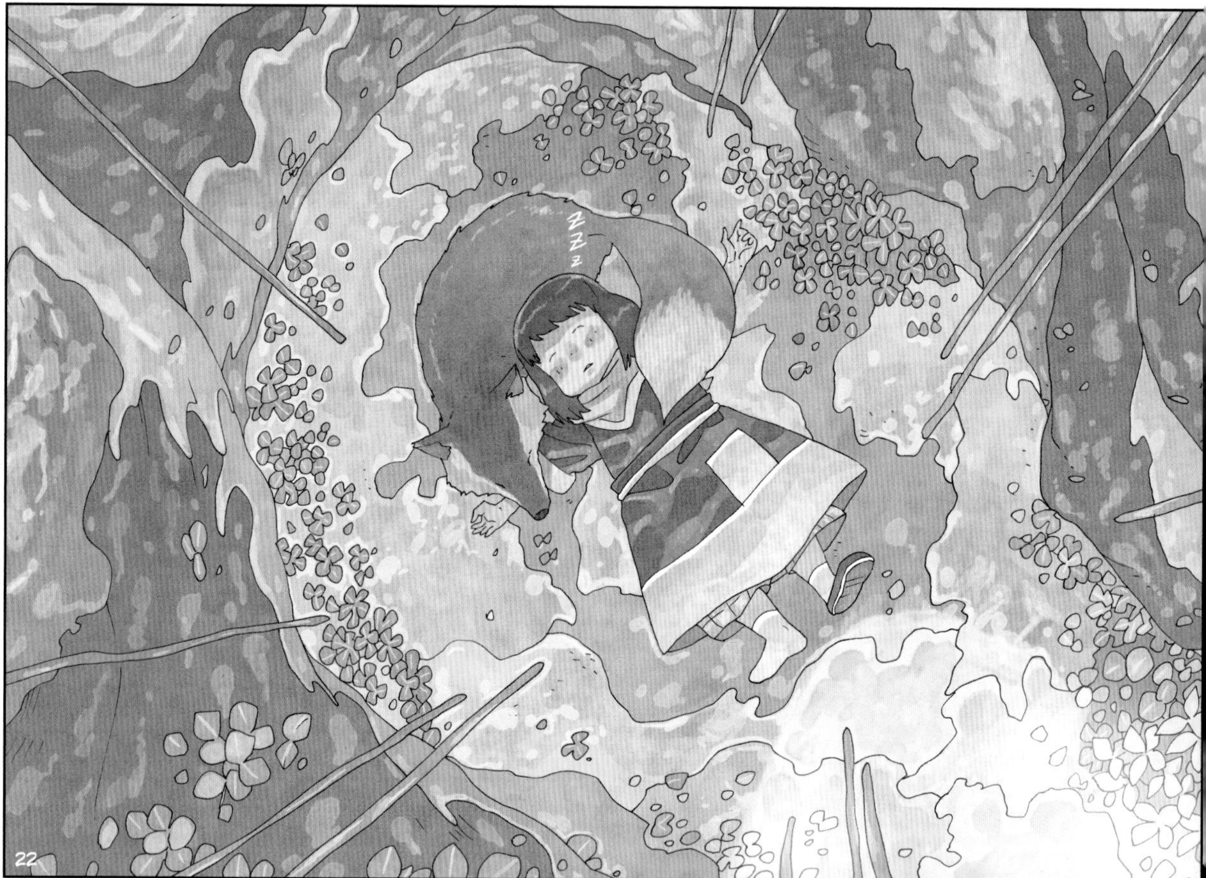
Z Z z

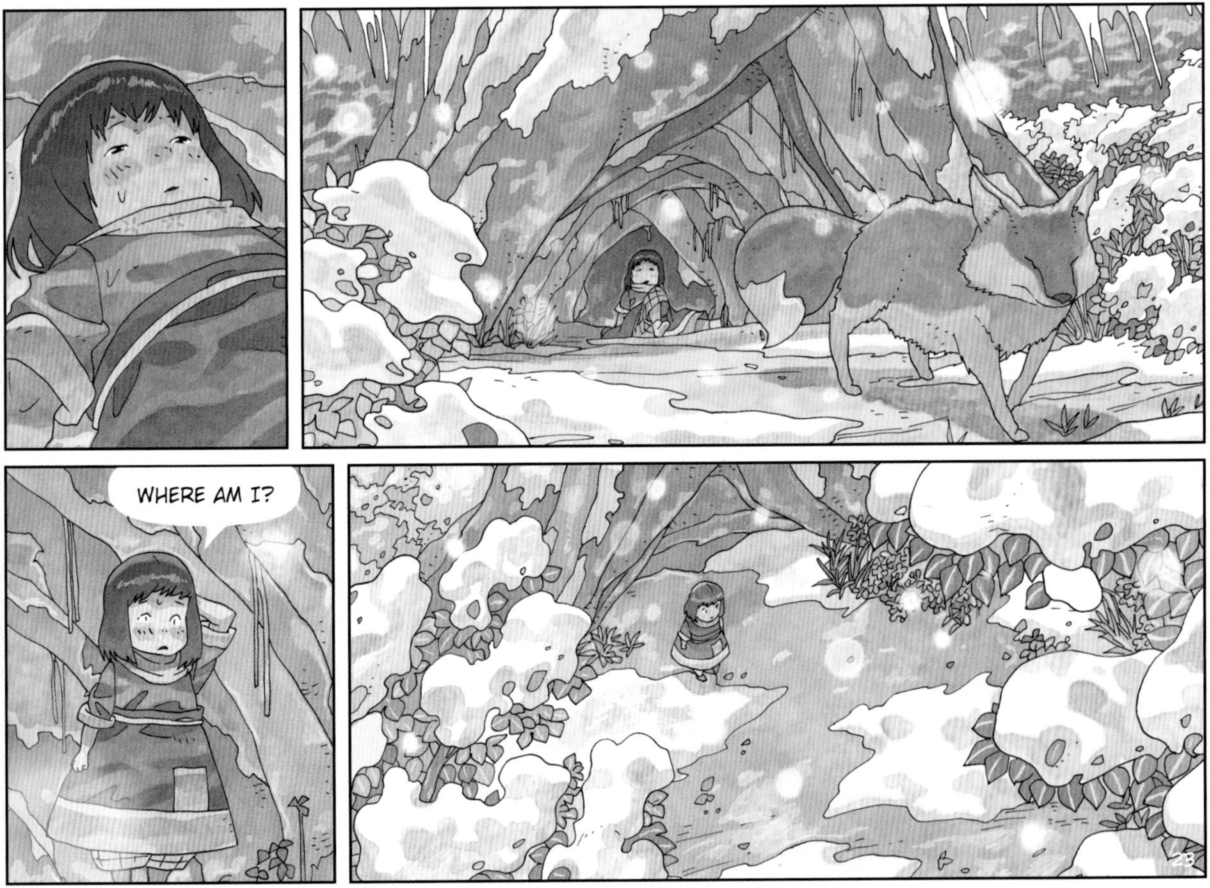
WHERE AM I?

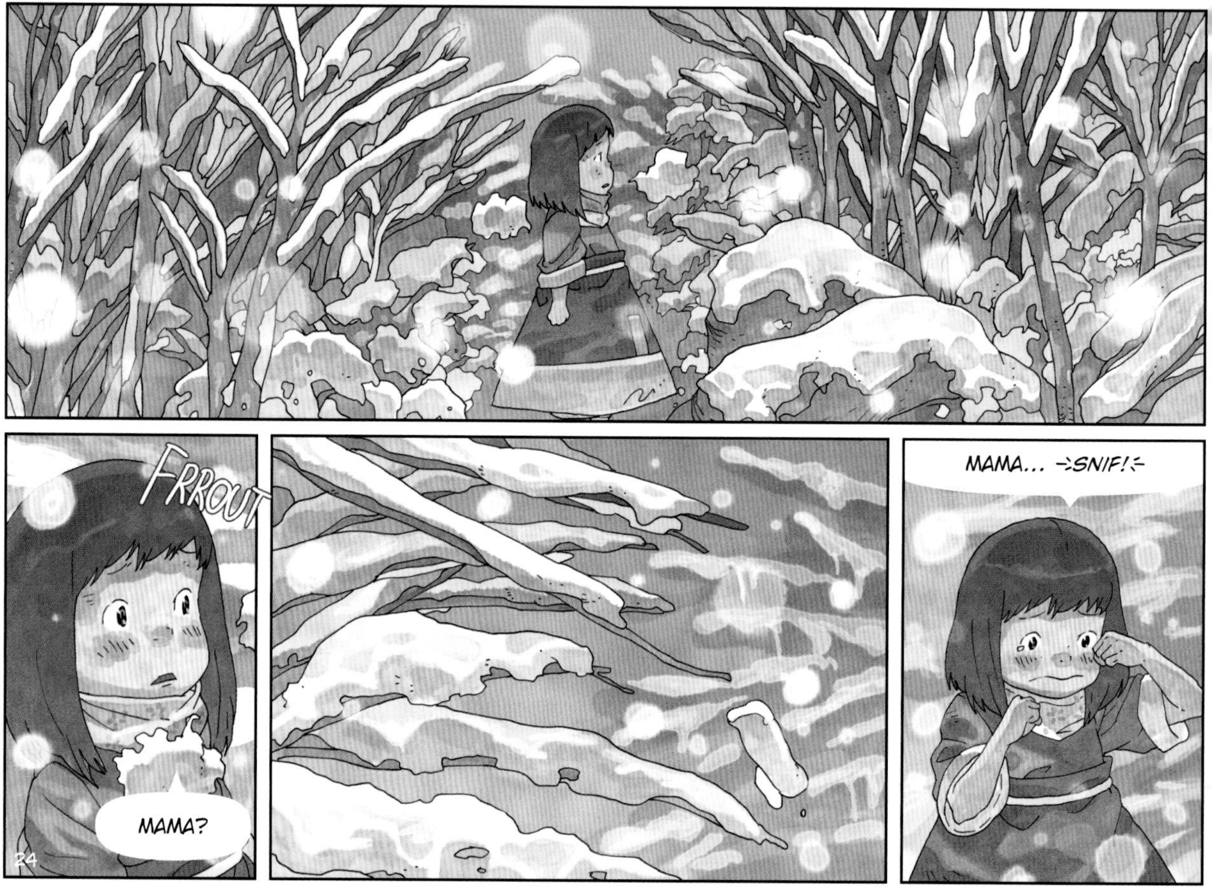
FRROUT
MAMA?
MAMA... -SNIF!-

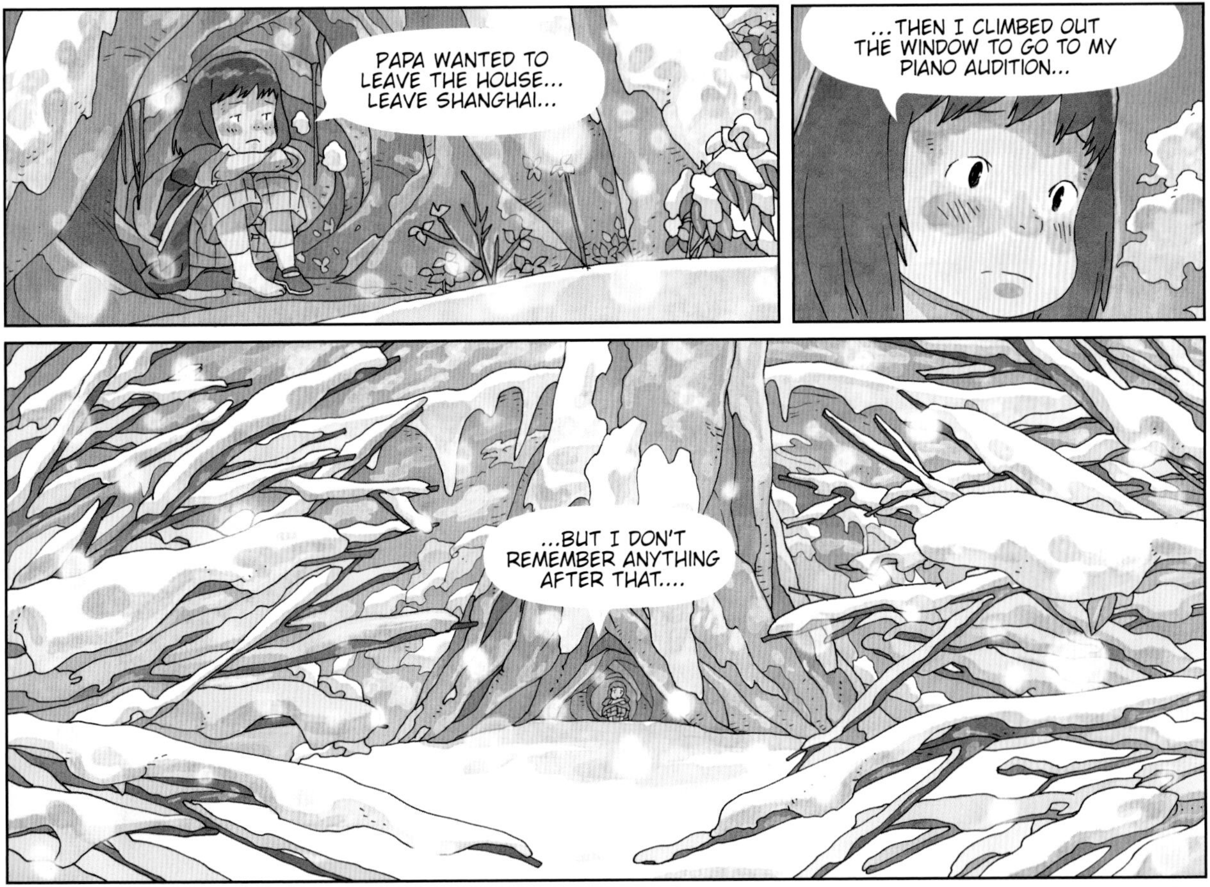
PAPA WANTED TO LEAVE THE HOUSE... LEAVE SHANGHAI...
...THEN I CLIMBED OUT THE WINDOW TO GO TO MY PIANO AUDITION...
...BUT I DON'T REMEMBER ANYTHING AFTER THAT....

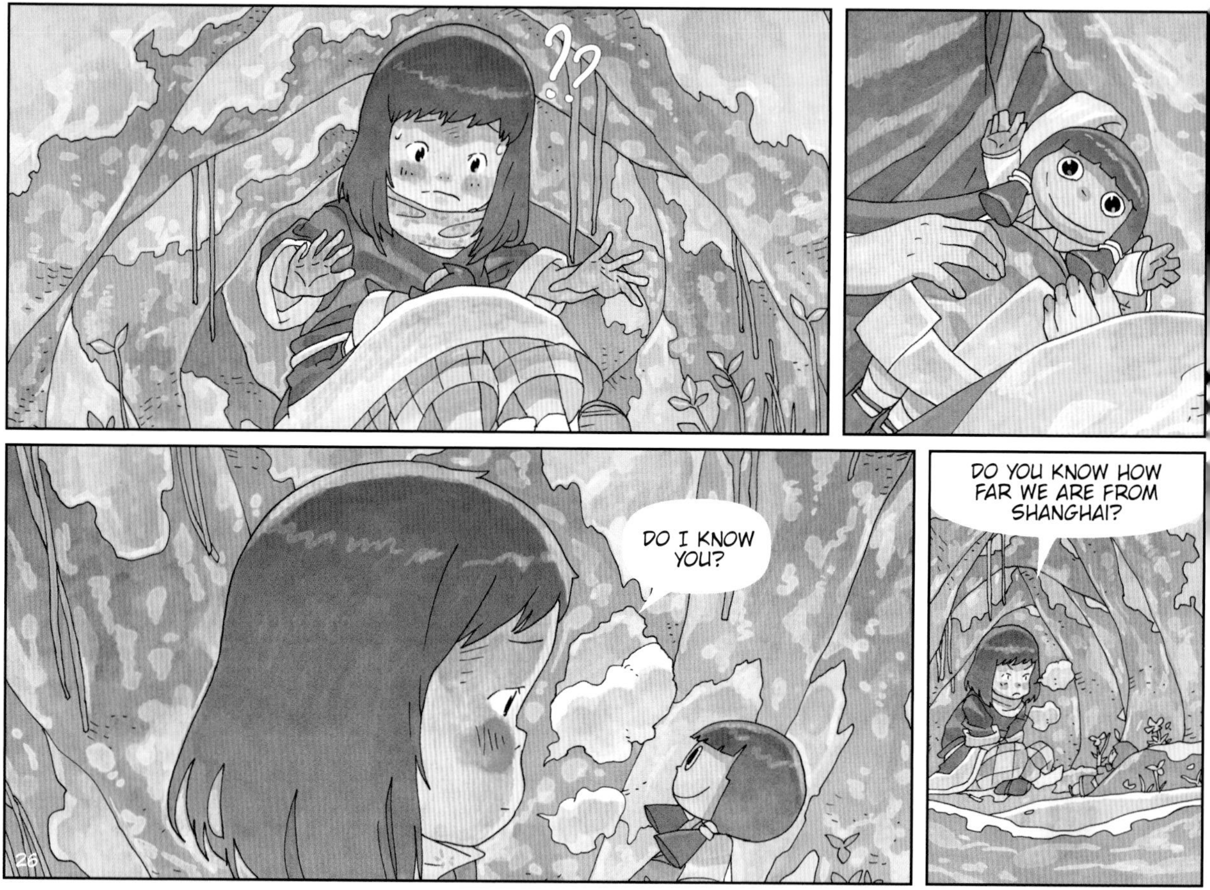
??
DO I KNOW YOU?
DO YOU KNOW HOW FAR WE ARE FROM SHANGHAI?

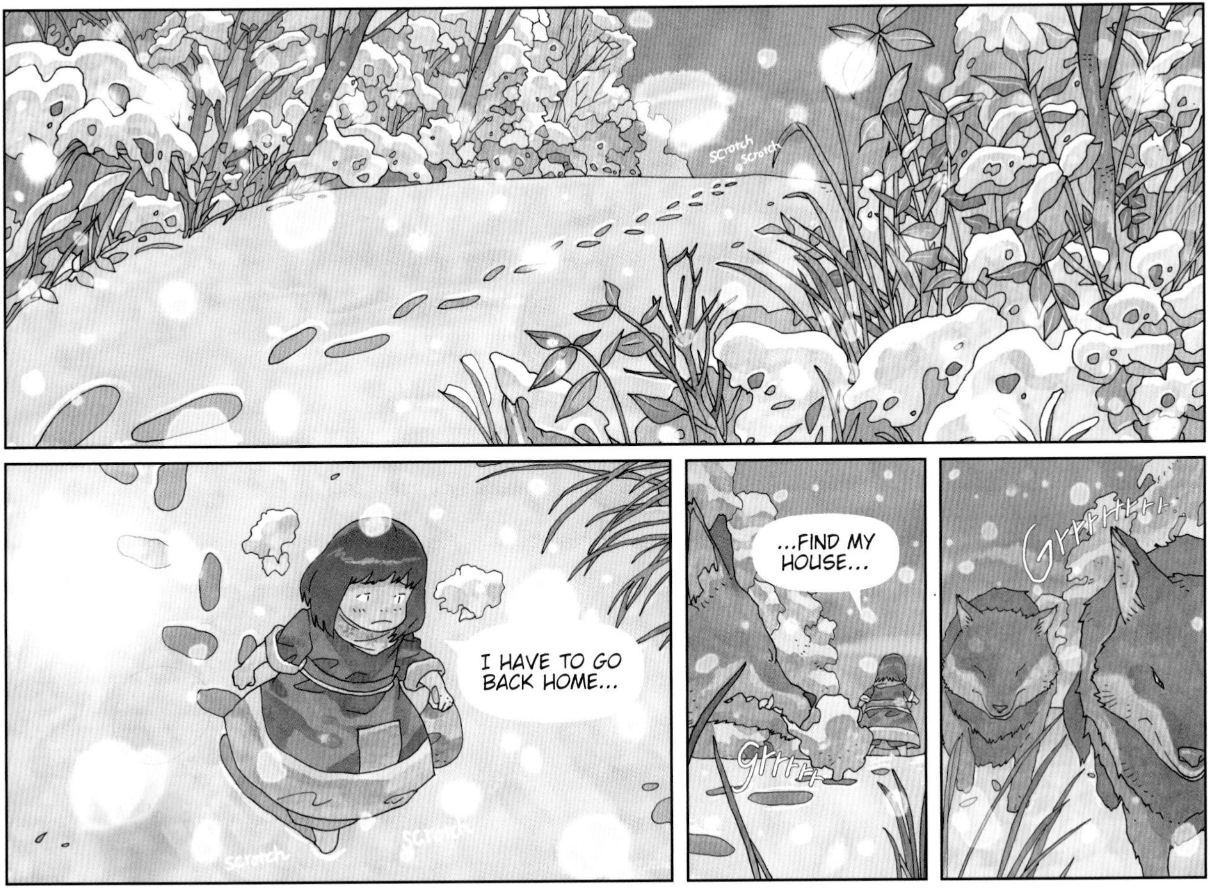
SCRATCH SCRATCH
I HAVE TO GO BACK HOME...
SCRATCH
SCRATCH
...FIND MY HOUSE...
GRRRRR
GRRRRRRRR...

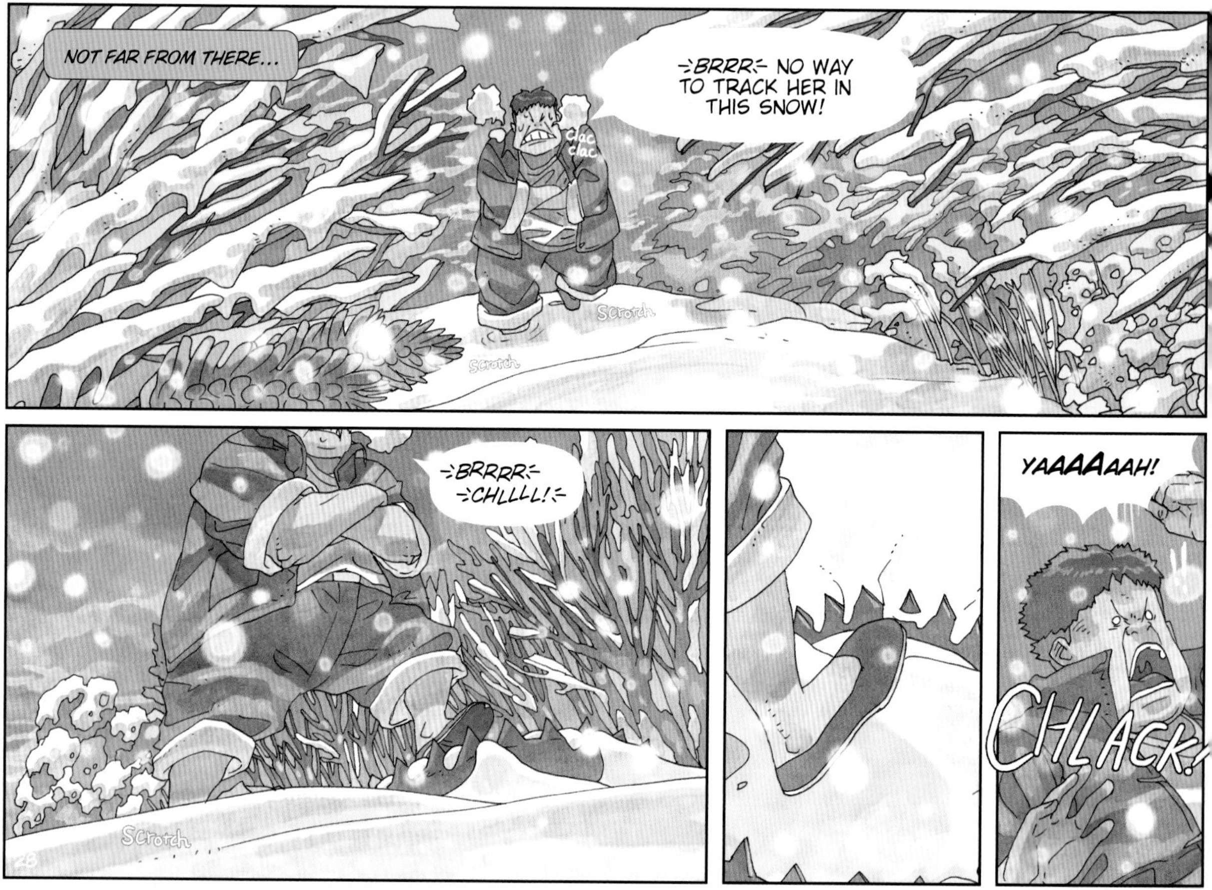

NOT FAR FROM THERE...
-BRRR- NO WAY TO TRACK HER IN THIS SNOW!
clac clac
SCROTCH
SCROTCH
-BRRRR- -CHLLLL!-
SCROTCH
YAAAAAAH!
CHLACK!

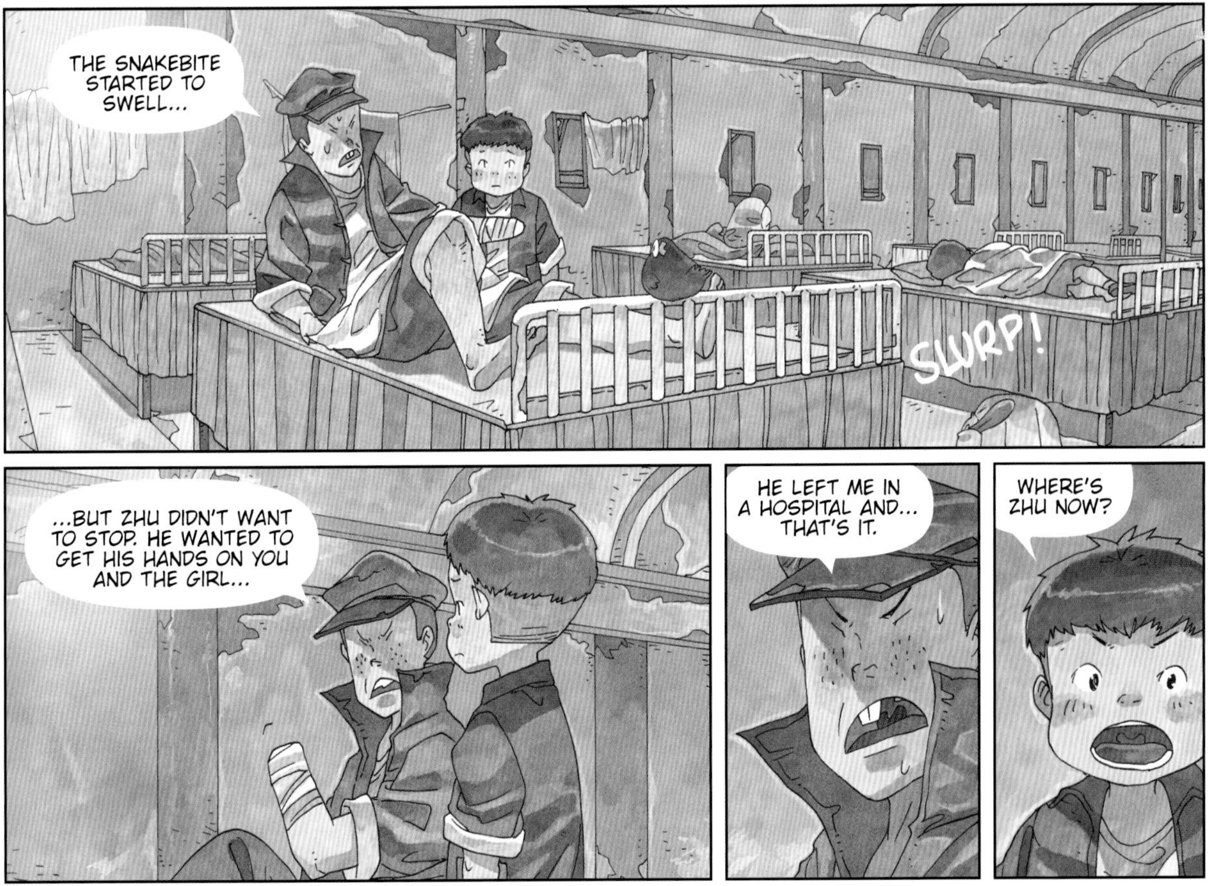
THE SNAKEBITE STARTED TO SWELL...
SLURP!
...BUT ZHU DIDN'T WANT TO STOP. HE WANTED TO GET HIS HANDS ON YOU AND THE GIRL...
HE LEFT ME IN A HOSPITAL AND... THAT'S IT.
WHERE'S ZHU NOW?

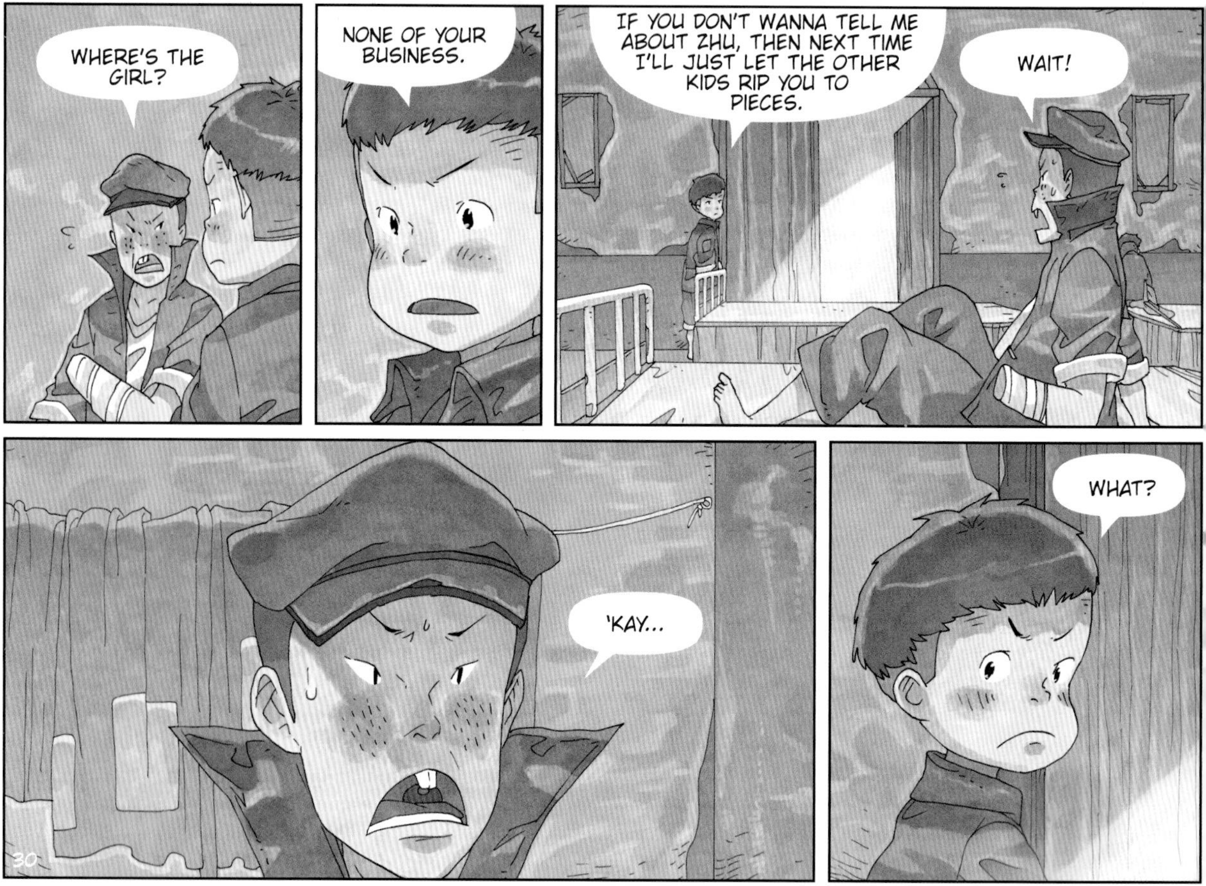
WHERE'S THE GIRL?
NONE OF YOUR BUSINESS.
IF YOU DON'T WANNA TELL ME ABOUT ZHU, THEN NEXT TIME I'LL JUST LET THE OTHER KIDS RIP YOU TO PIECES.
WAIT!
'KAY...
WHAT?

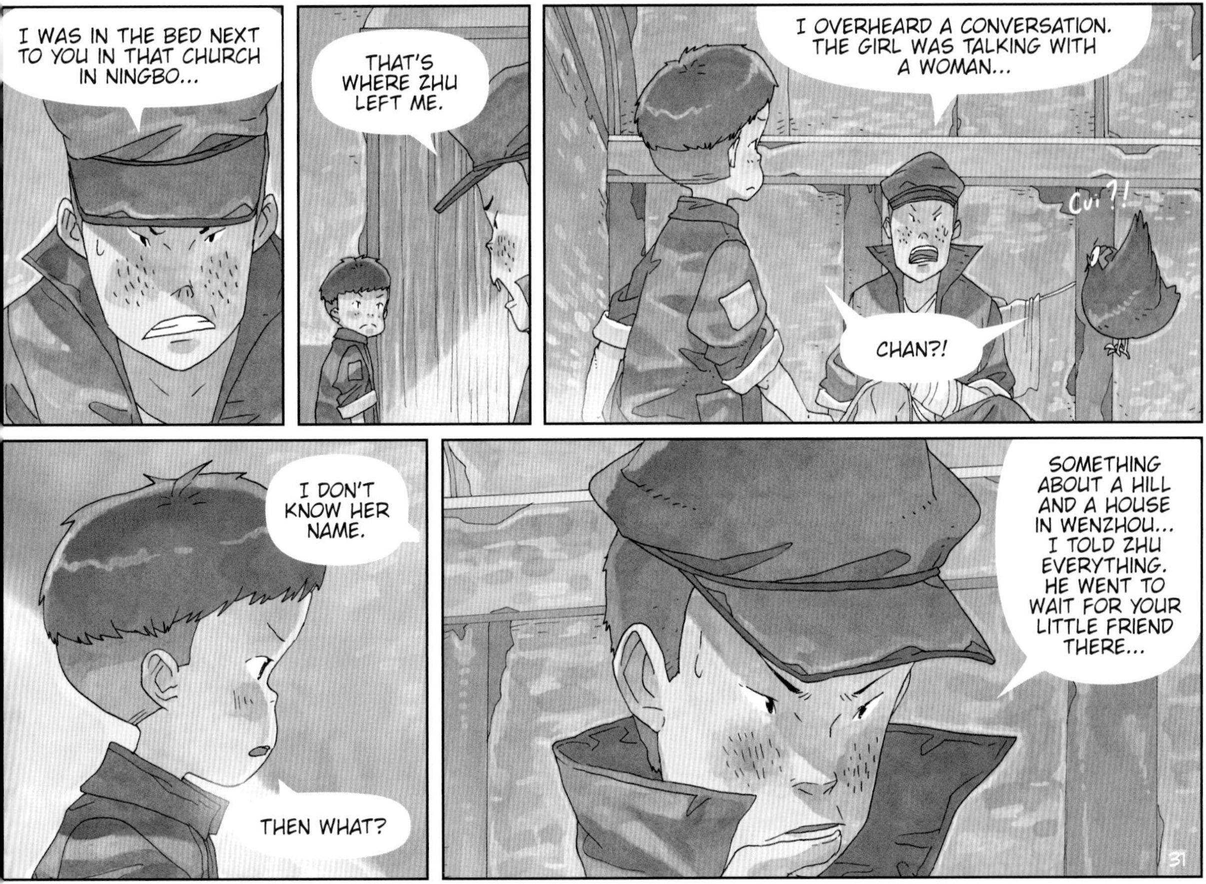

I WAS IN THE BED NEXT TO YOU IN THAT CHURCH IN NINGBO...
THAT'S WHERE ZHU LEFT ME.
I OVERHEARD A CONVERSATION. THE GIRL WAS TALKING WITH A WOMAN...
CHAN?!
Cui?!
I DON'T KNOW HER NAME.
THEN WHAT?
SOMETHING ABOUT A HILL AND A HOUSE IN WENZHOU... I TOLD ZHU EVERYTHING. HE WENT TO WAIT FOR YOUR LITTLE FRIEND THERE...

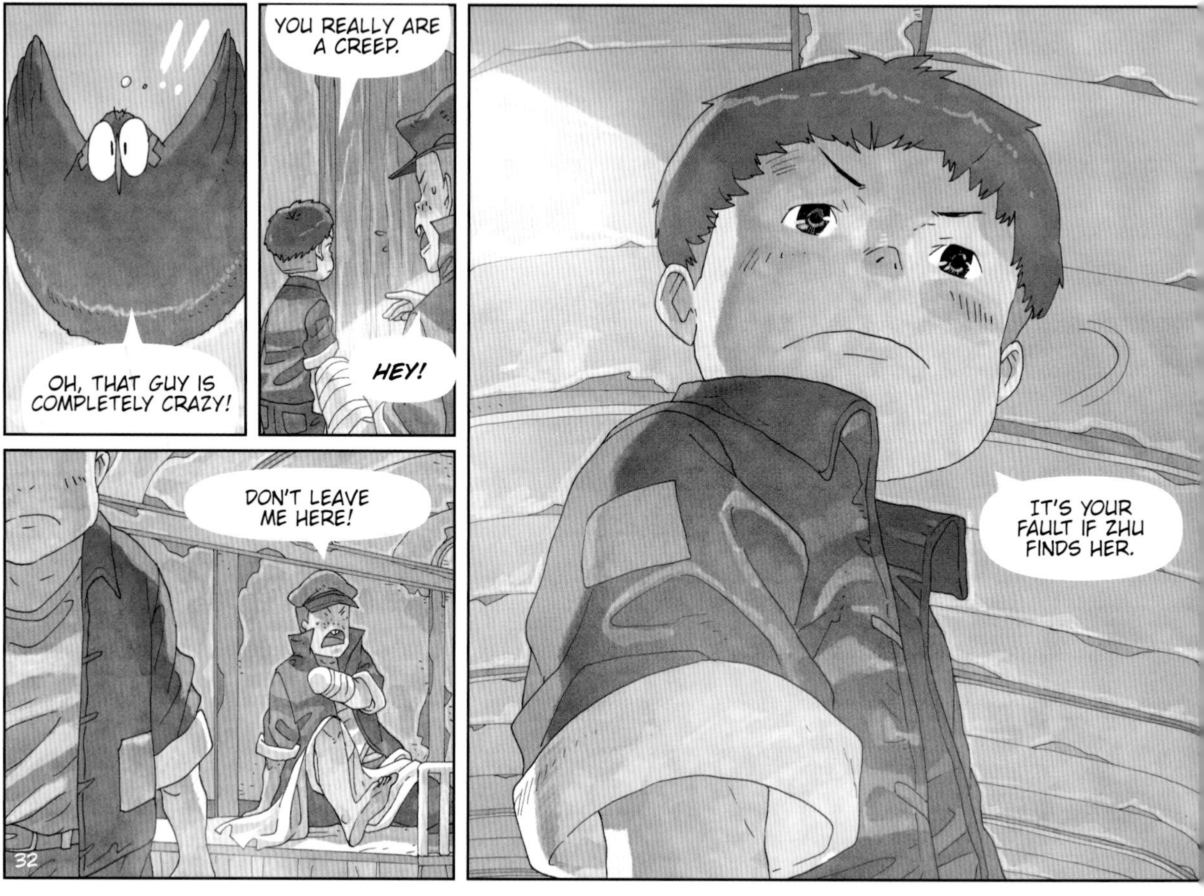
!!
OH, THAT GUY IS COMPLETELY CRAZY!
YOU REALLY ARE A CREEP.
HEY!
DON'T LEAVE ME HERE!
IT'S YOUR FAULT IF ZHU FINDS HER.

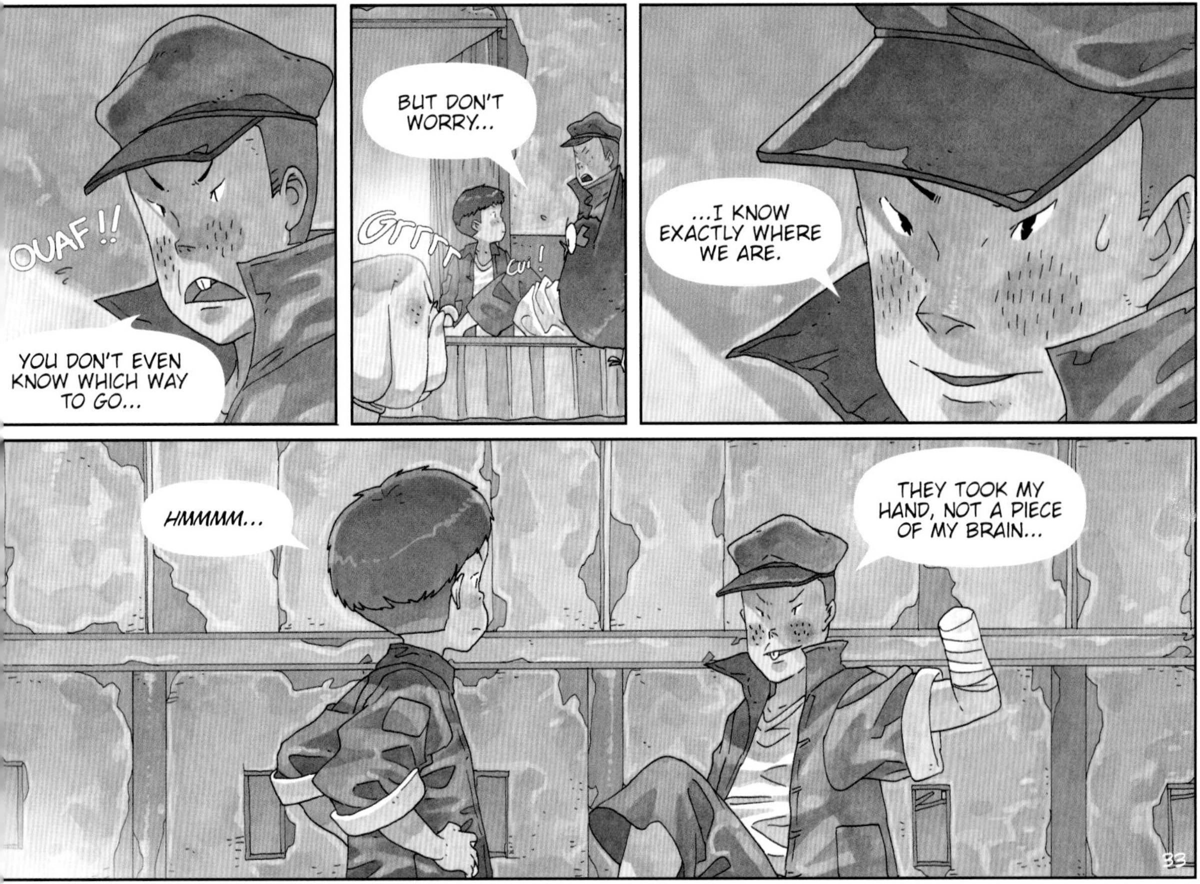
OUAF !!
YOU DON'T EVEN KNOW WHICH WAY TO GO...
BUT DON'T WORRY...
Grrrr
Cui !
...I KNOW EXACTLY WHERE WE ARE.
HMMMM...
THEY TOOK MY HAND, NOT A PIECE OF MY BRAIN...

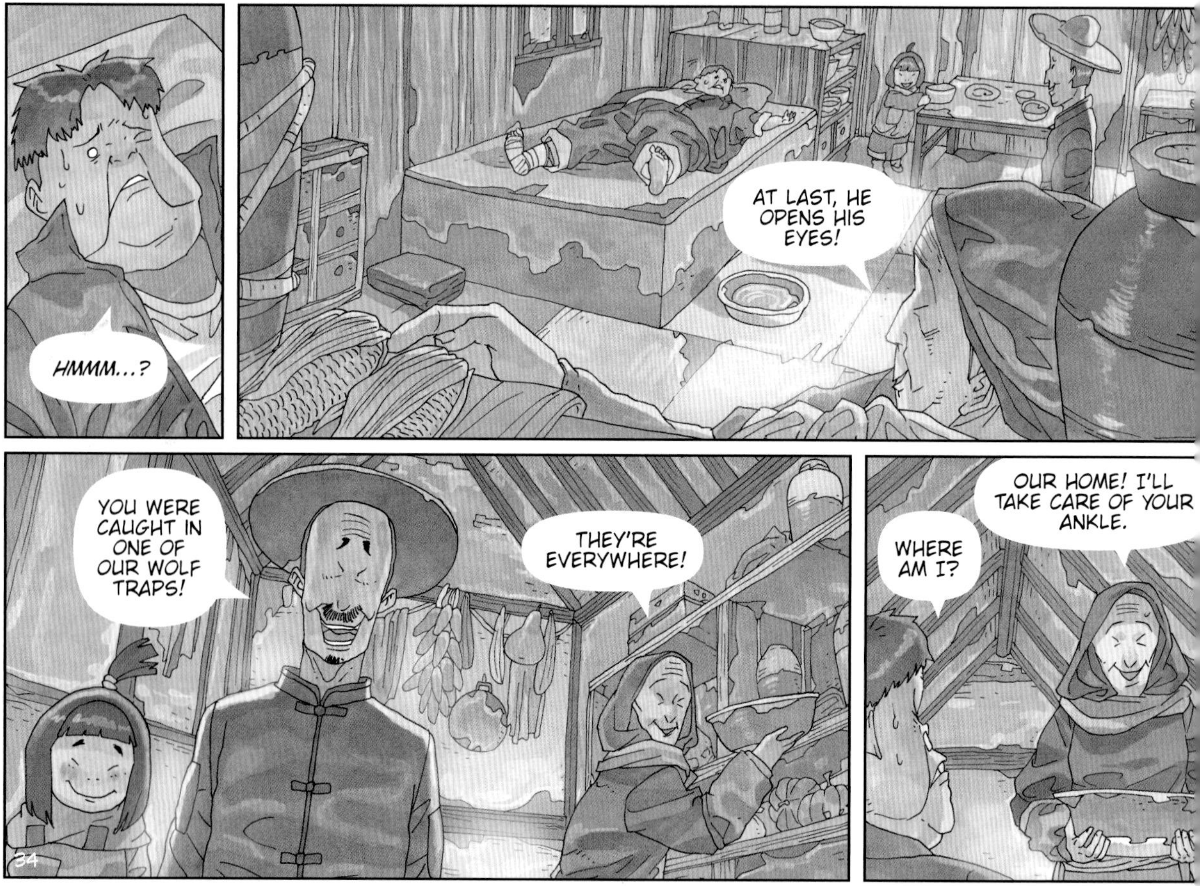
HMMM...?
AT LAST, HE OPENS HIS EYES!
YOU WERE CAUGHT IN ONE OF OUR WOLF TRAPS!
THEY'RE EVERYWHERE!
WHERE AM I?
OUR HOME! I'LL TAKE CARE OF YOUR ANKLE.

HUMF... I GOTTA GO.

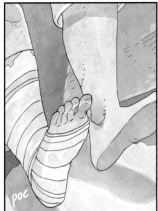

POC

RHAAAA!

YOU WON'T GET TEN FEET IN THE STATE YOU'RE IN...

LISTEN TO MY HUSBAND. BE REASONABLE.

BESIDES, THERE'S A SNOWSTORM COMING. YOU'LL BE BETTER OFF HERE WITH US.

35

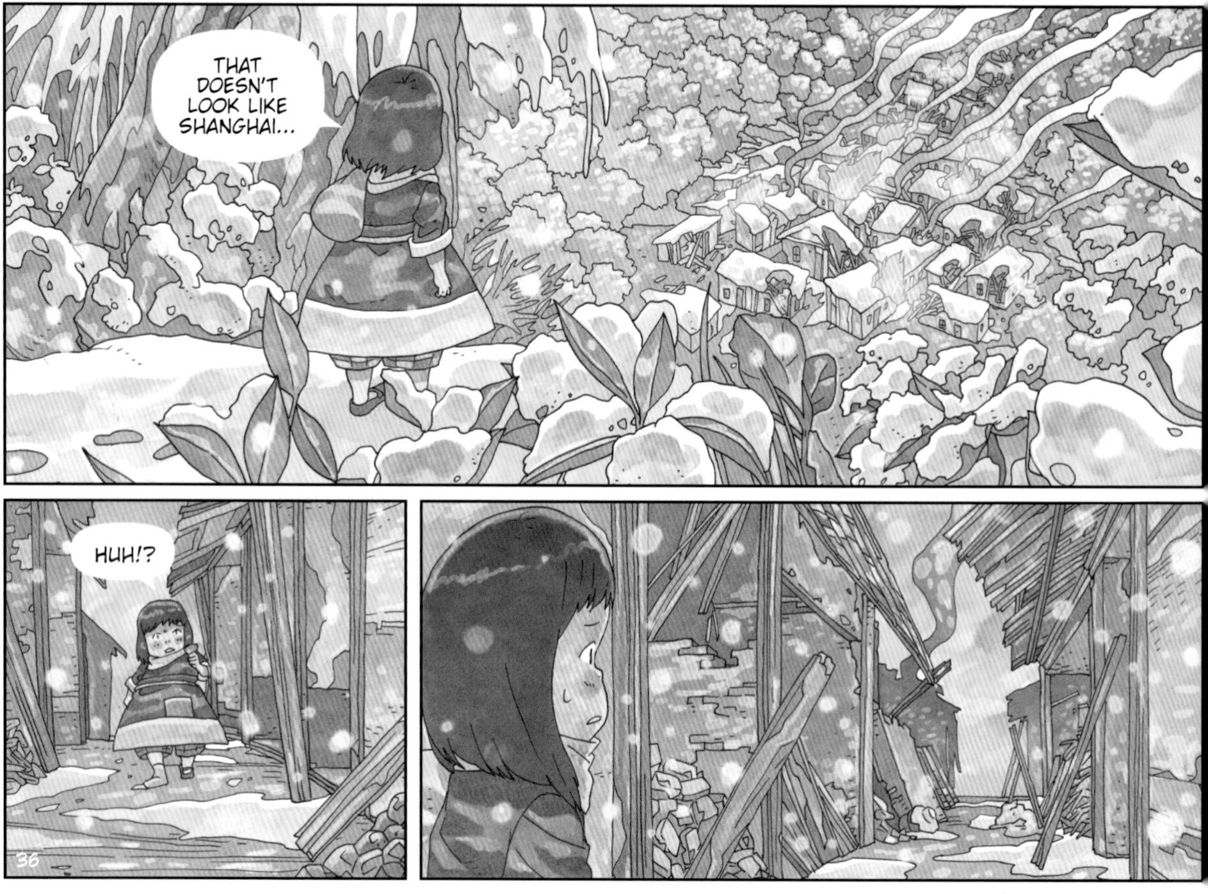
THAT DOESN'T LOOK LIKE SHANGHAI...
HUH!?

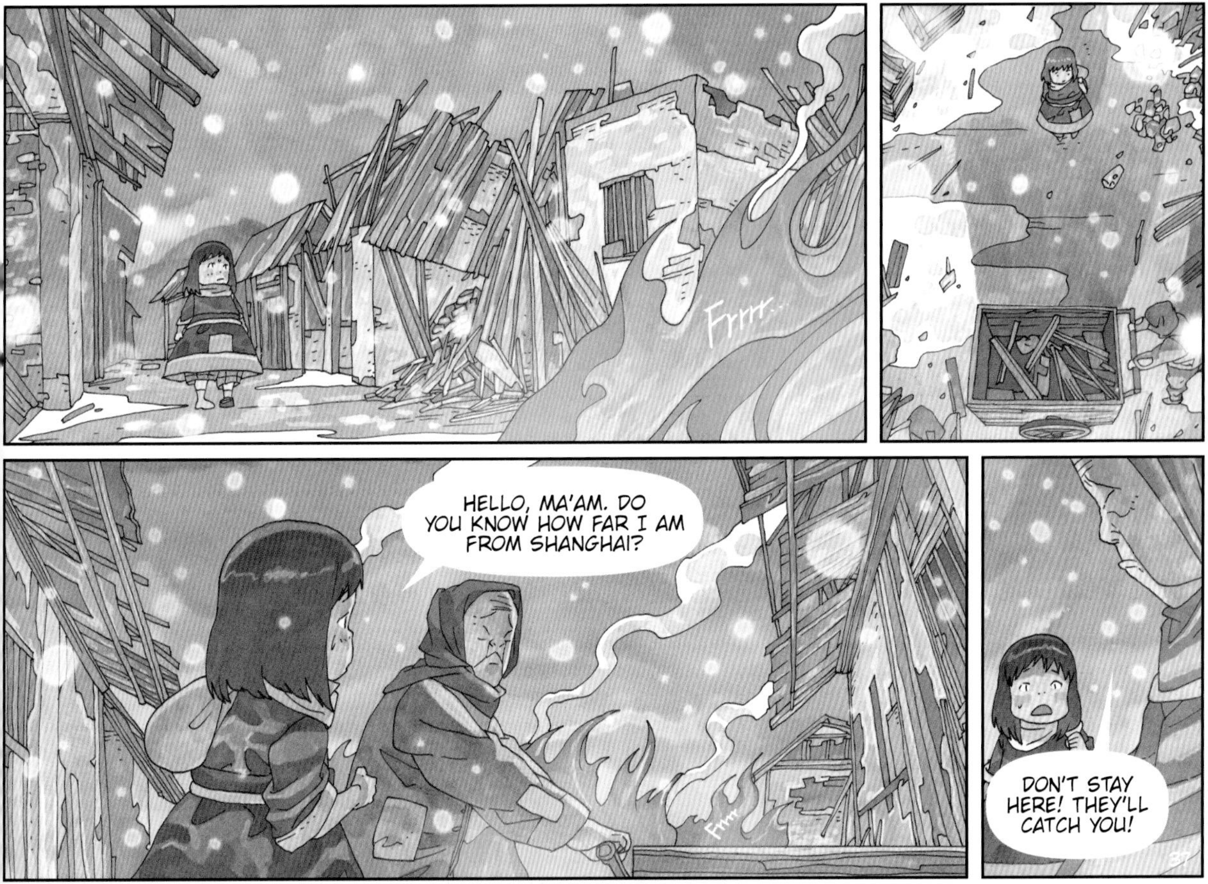
Frrrr...
HELLO, MA'AM. DO YOU KNOW HOW FAR I AM FROM SHANGHAI?
Frrr
DON'T STAY HERE! THEY'LL CATCH YOU!

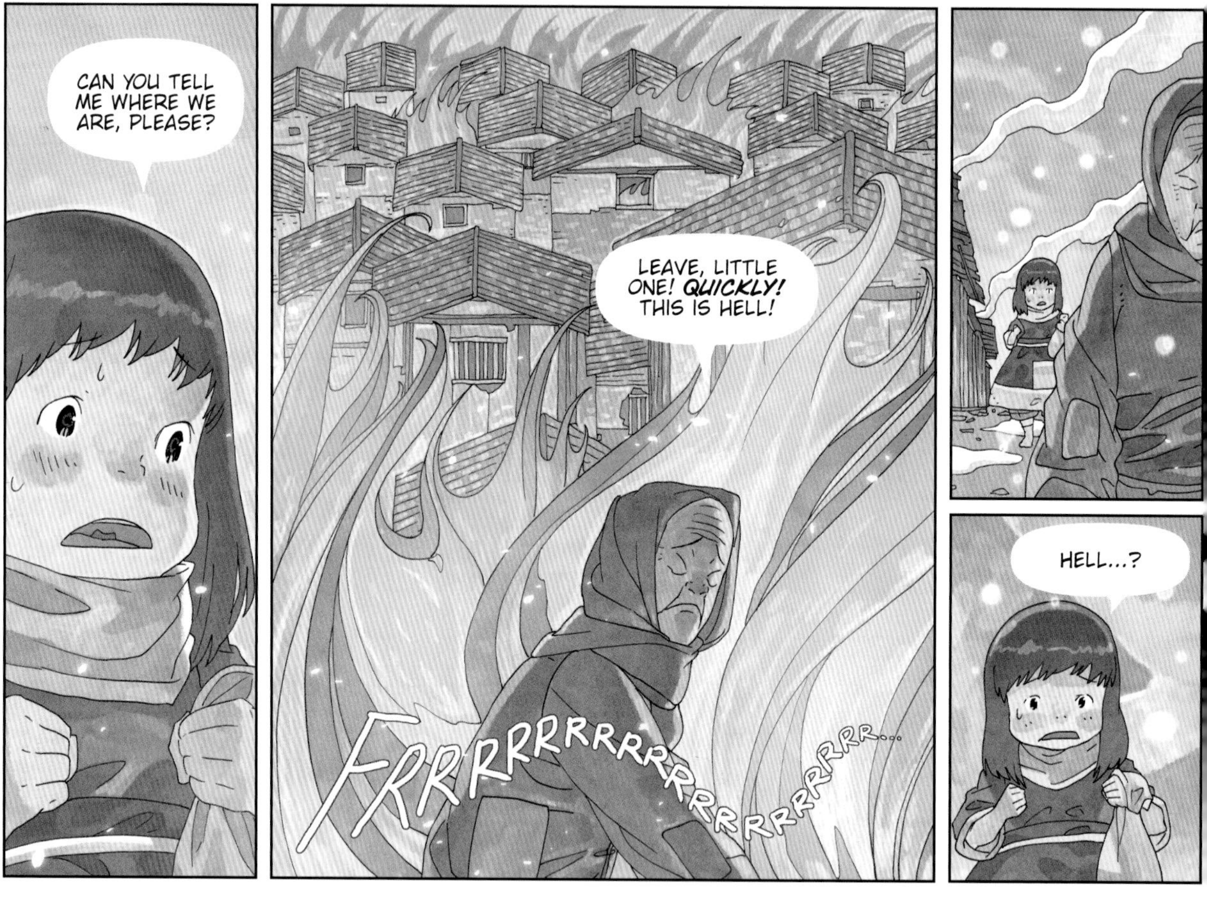
CAN YOU TELL ME WHERE WE ARE, PLEASE?
LEAVE, LITTLE ONE! ***QUICKLY!*** THIS IS HELL!
FRRRRRRRRRRRRRRRRRRRRRRR...
HELL...?

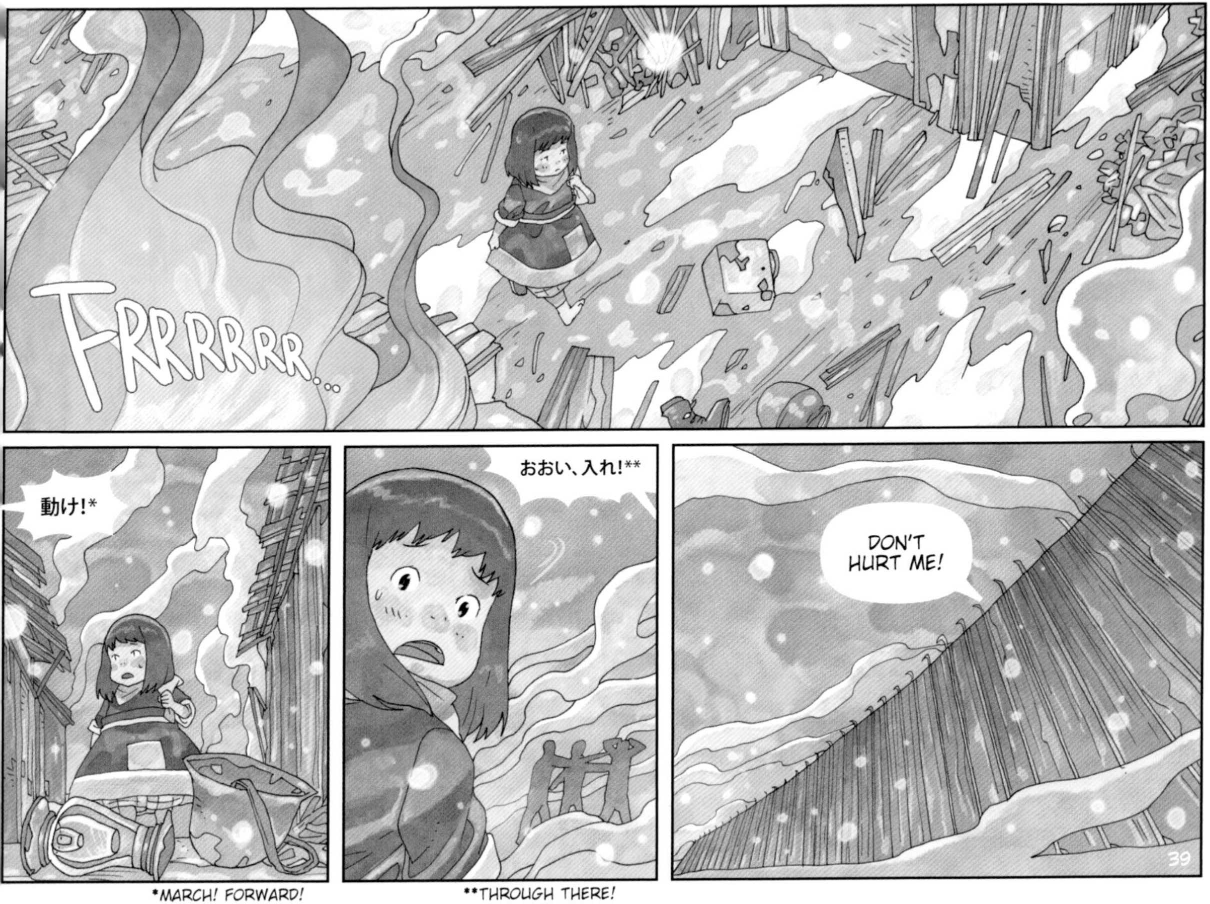
FRRRRRR...
動け!*
おおい、入れ!**
DON'T HURT ME!

*MARCH! FORWARD!

**THROUGH THERE!

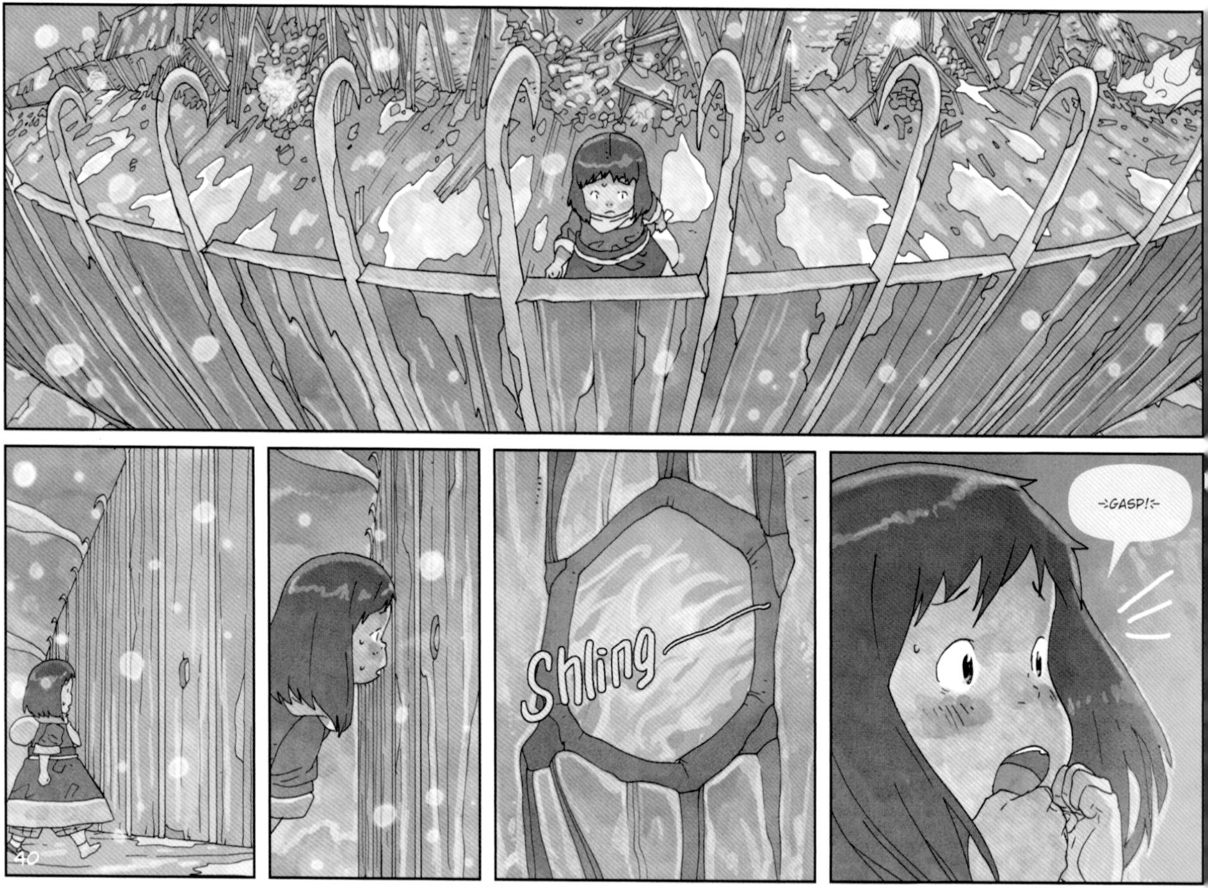
Shling
-GASP!-

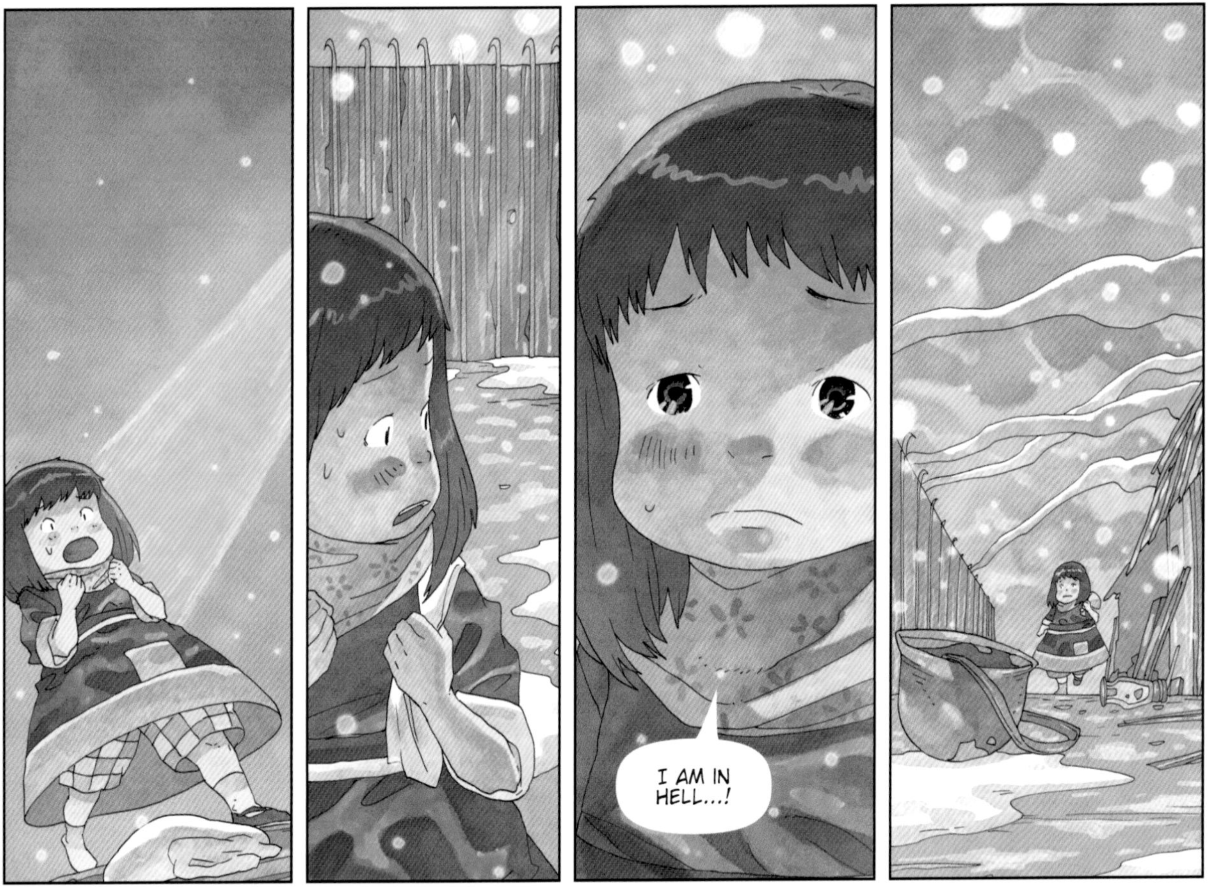
I AM IN HELL...!

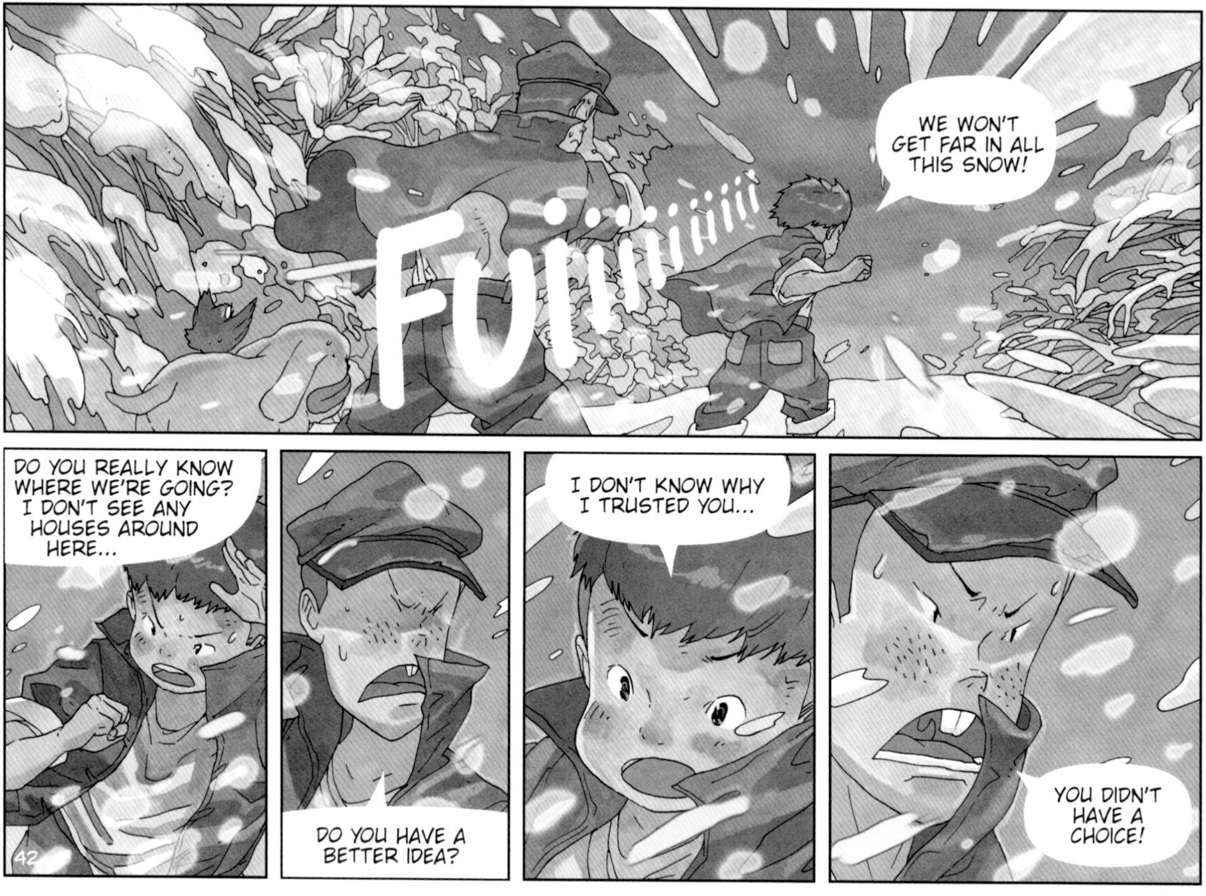
WE WON'T GET FAR IN ALL THIS SNOW!
FUIiiiiiiiiii
DO YOU REALLY KNOW WHERE WE'RE GOING? I DON'T SEE ANY HOUSES AROUND HERE...
DO YOU HAVE A BETTER IDEA?
I DON'T KNOW WHY I TRUSTED YOU...
YOU DIDN'T HAVE A CHOICE!

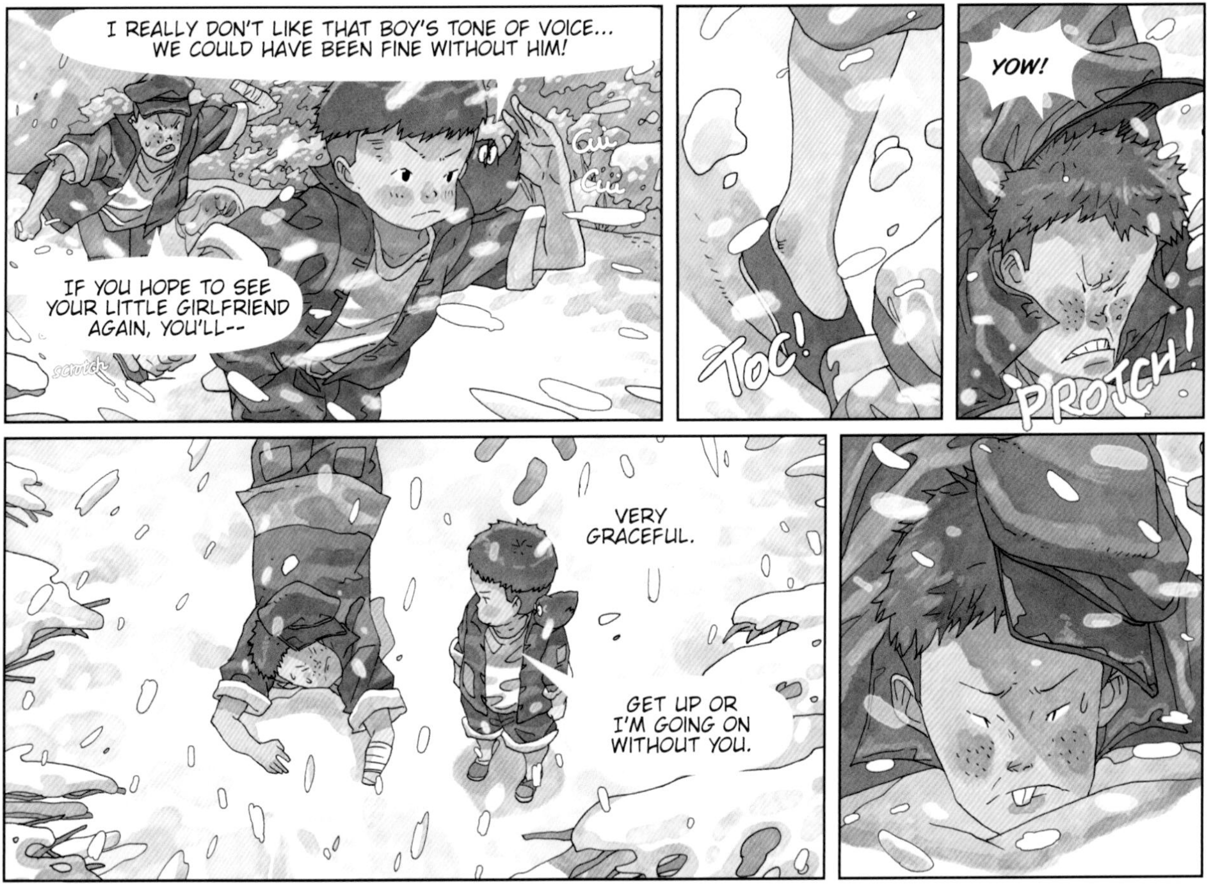

I REALLY DON'T LIKE THAT BOY'S TONE OF VOICE... WE COULD HAVE BEEN FINE WITHOUT HIM!
Cui Cui
IF YOU HOPE TO SEE YOUR LITTLE GIRLFRIEND AGAIN, YOU'LL--
scratch
TOC!
YOW!
PROTCH!
VERY GRACEFUL.
GET UP OR I'M GOING ON WITHOUT YOU.

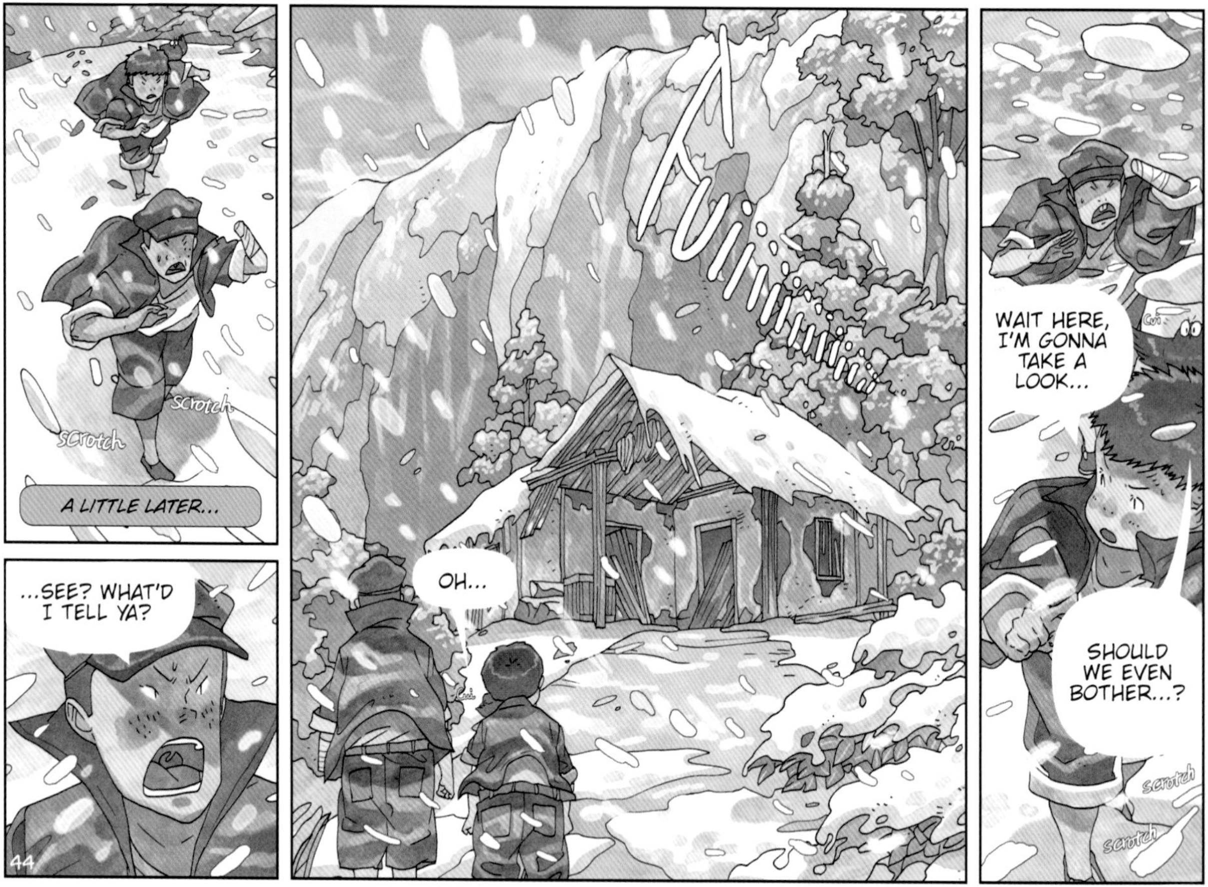

scrotch
scrotch
A LITTLE LATER...
...SEE? WHAT'D I TELL YA?
Fuiiiiiiiiiii
OH...
Cui
WAIT HERE, I'M GONNA TAKE A LOOK...
Cui
SHOULD WE EVEN BOTHER...?
scrotch
scrotch

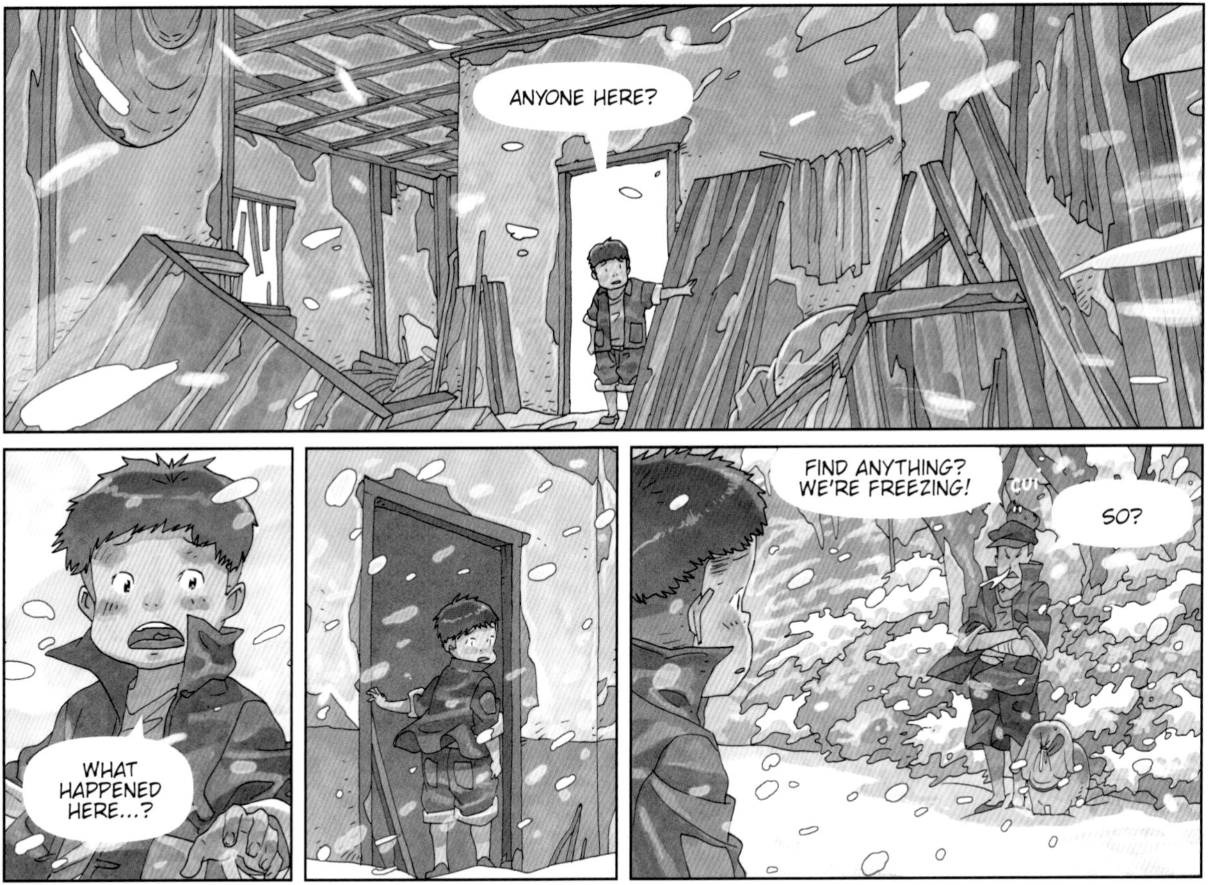
ANYONE HERE?
WHAT HAPPENED HERE...?
FIND ANYTHING? WE'RE FREEZING!
SO?

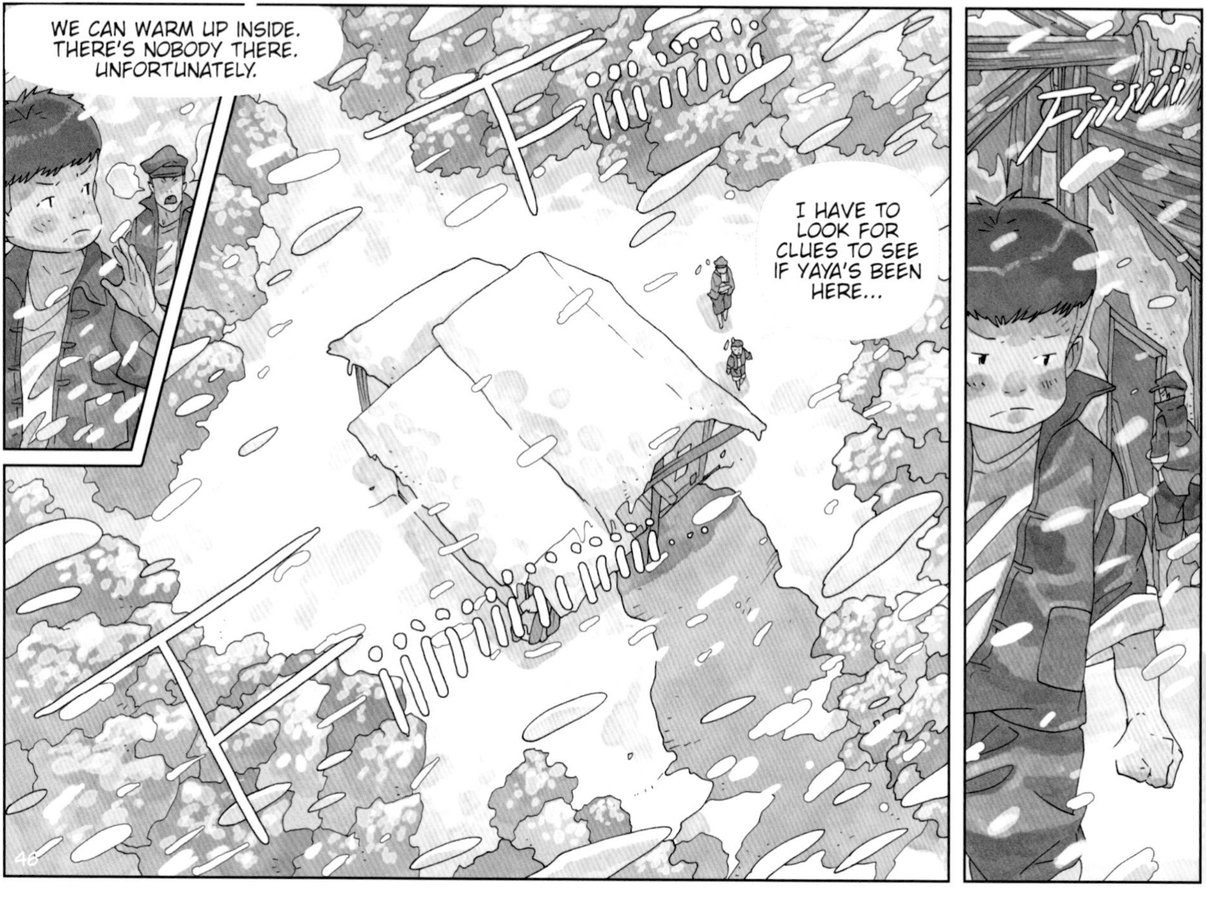
WE CAN WARM UP INSIDE. THERE'S NOBODY THERE. UNFORTUNATELY.
FFiiiiiiiii
I HAVE TO LOOK FOR CLUES TO SEE IF YAYA'S BEEN HERE...
FFiiiiiiiiiiiii
Fiiiiii

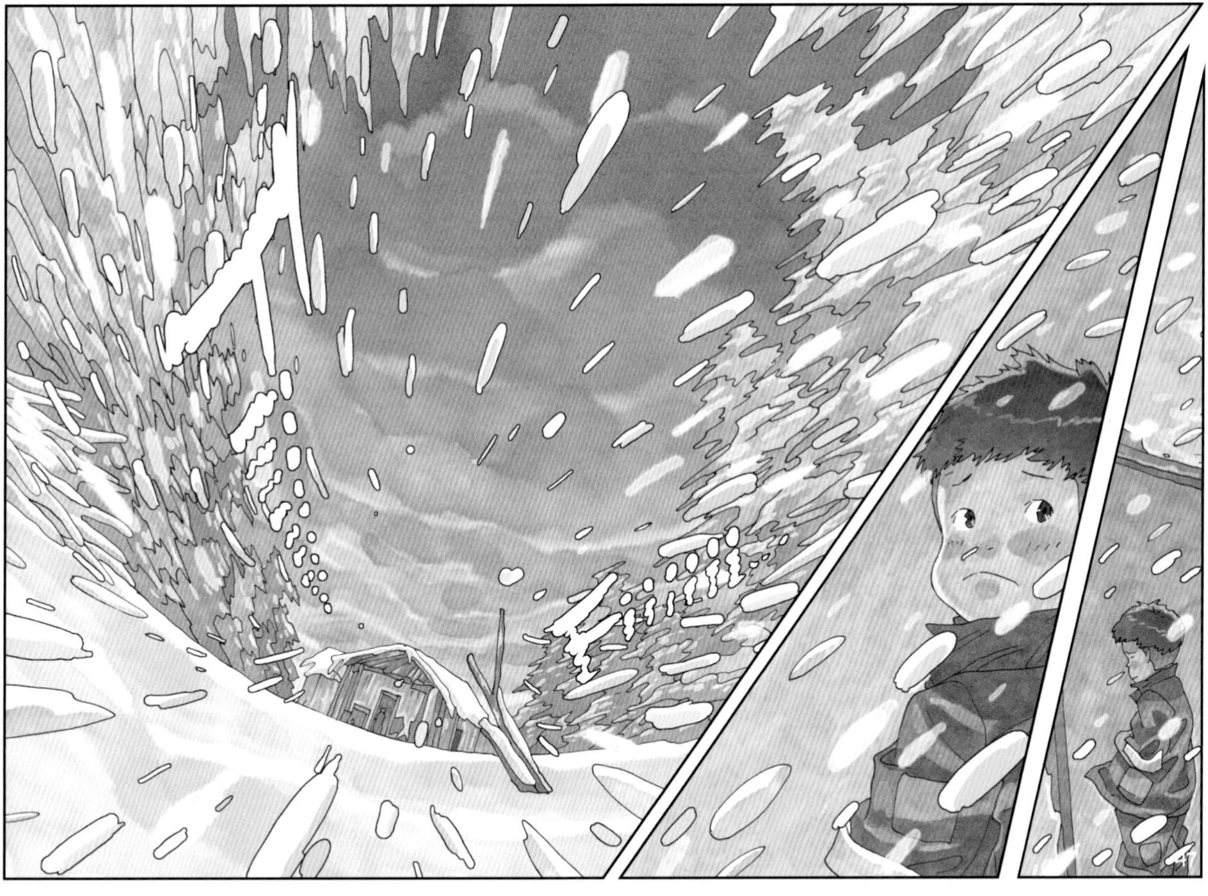

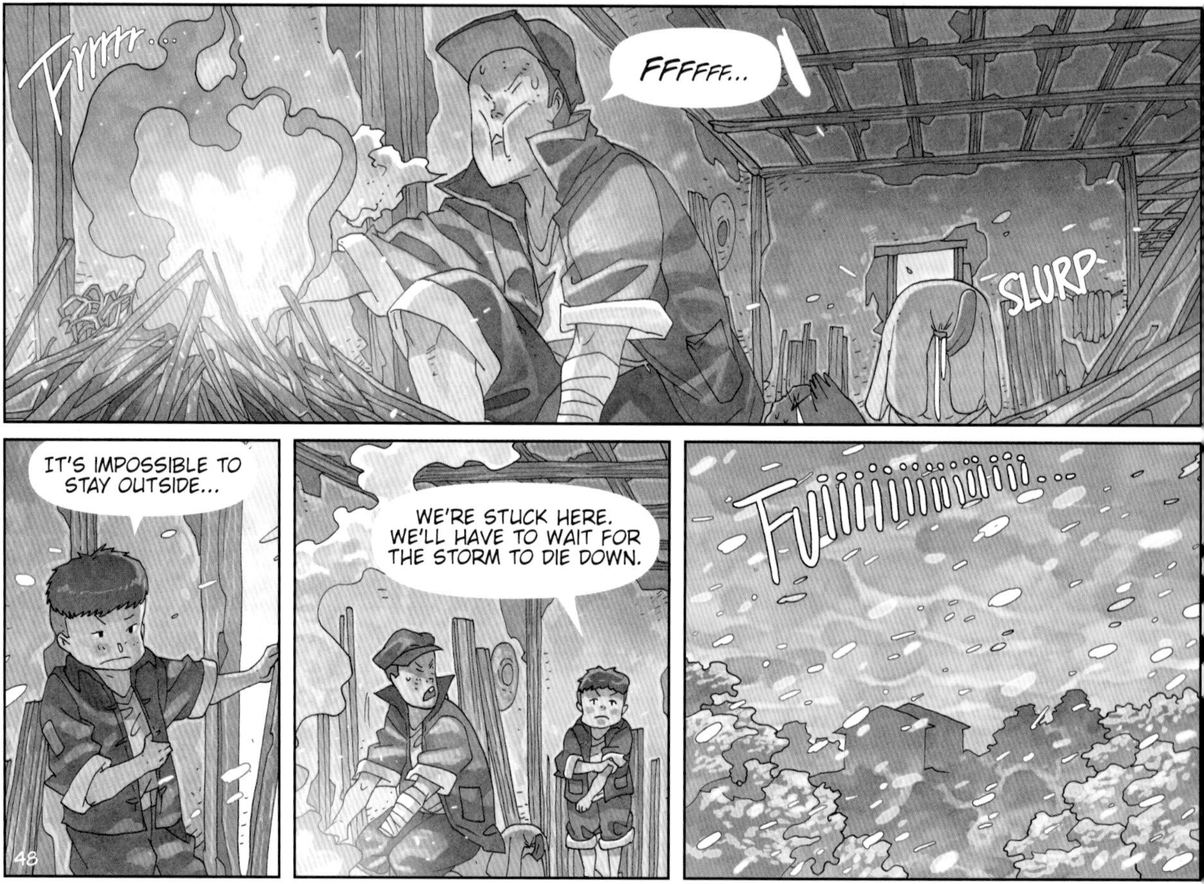

Frrrrr...
FFFFFF...
SLURP
IT'S IMPOSSIBLE TO STAY OUTSIDE...
WE'RE STUCK HERE. WE'LL HAVE TO WAIT FOR THE STORM TO DIE DOWN.
Fuiiiiiiiiiiiiii...

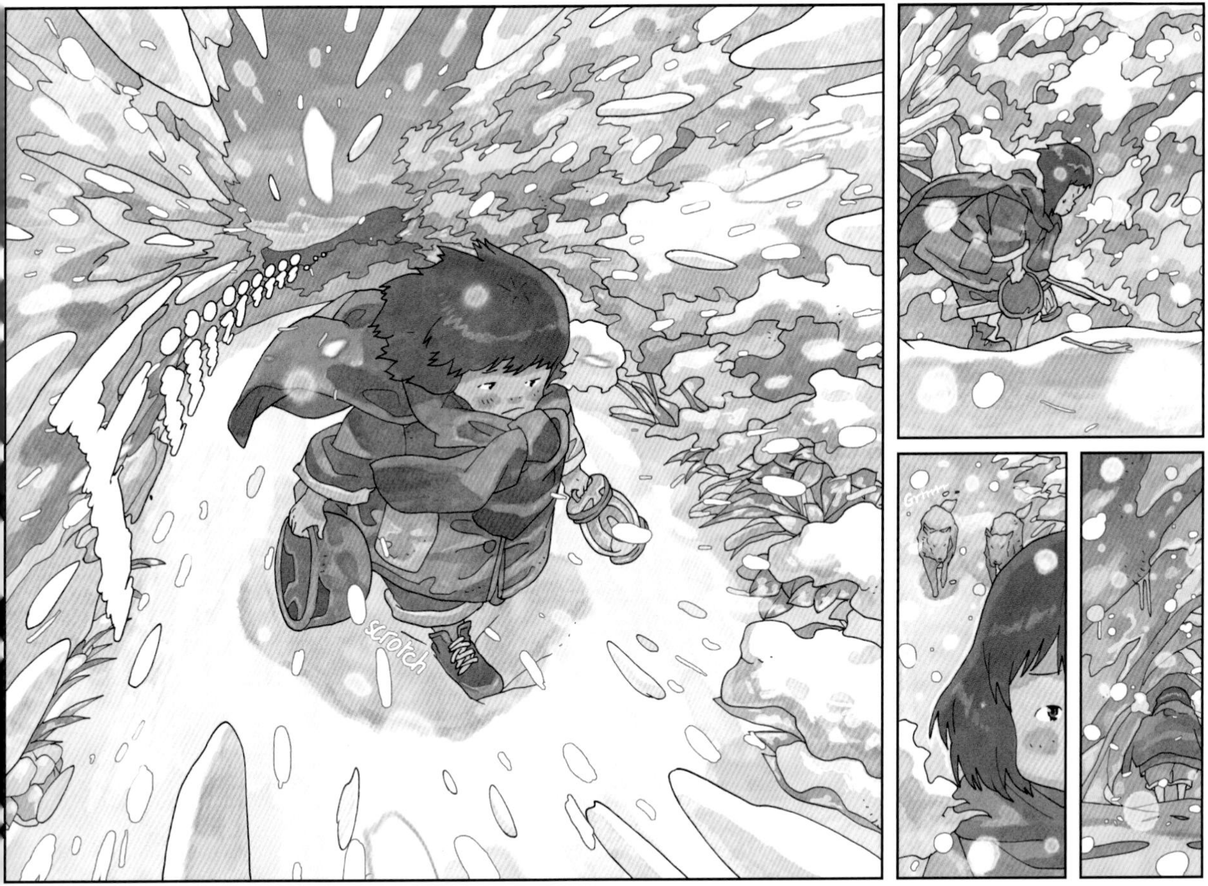
scrotch
Grrrr

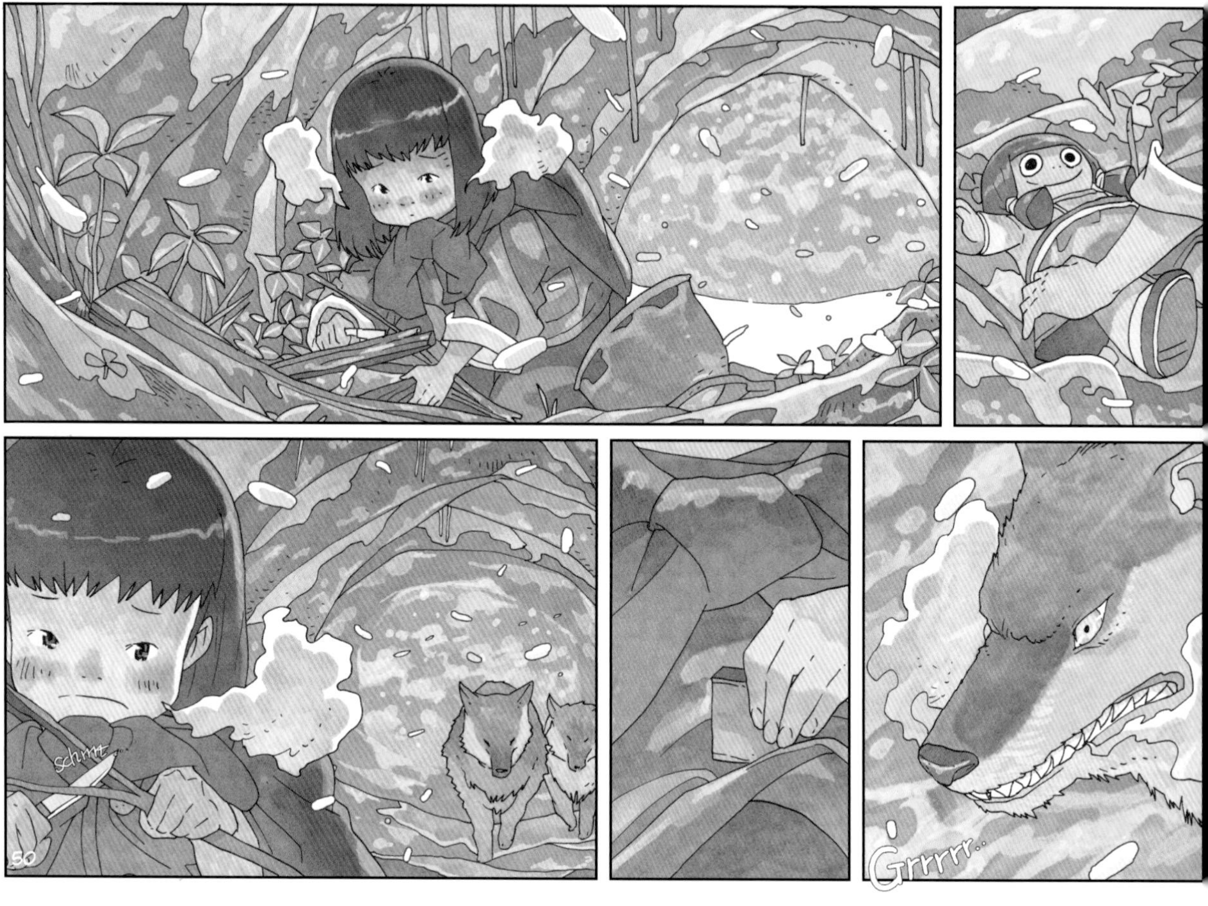
schrrrt
Grrrrr..

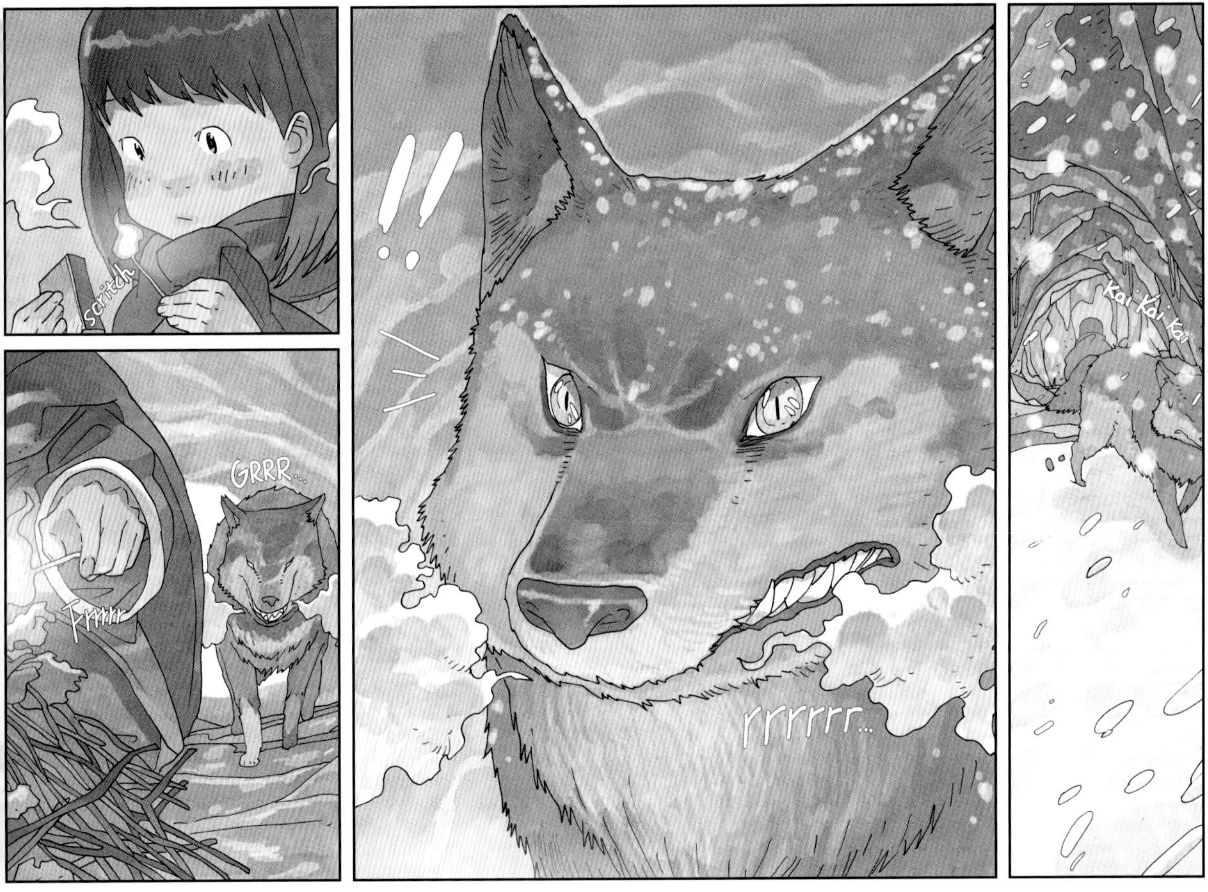
scritch
GRRR...
Frrrrr
!!
rrrrrr...
Kai Kai Kai

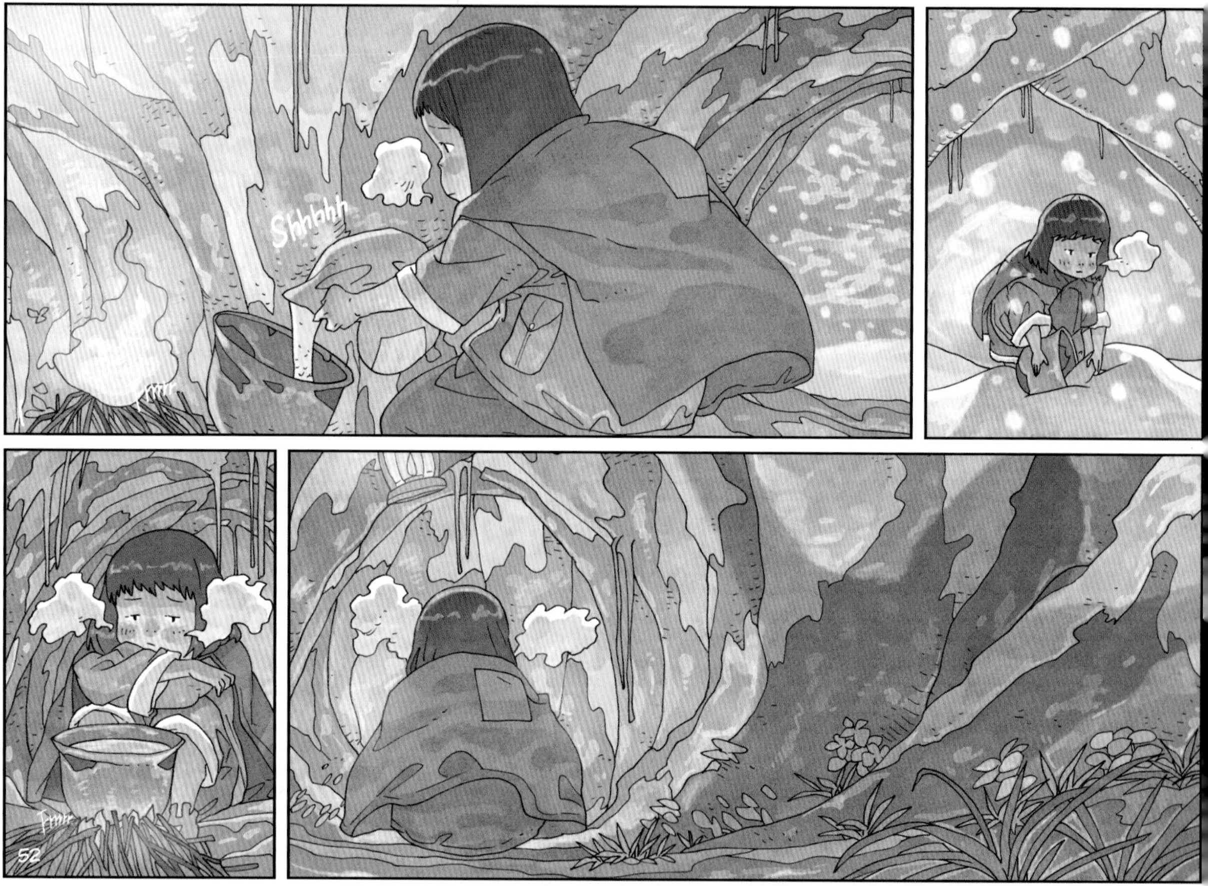
Shhhhh
Frrrr
Frrrr

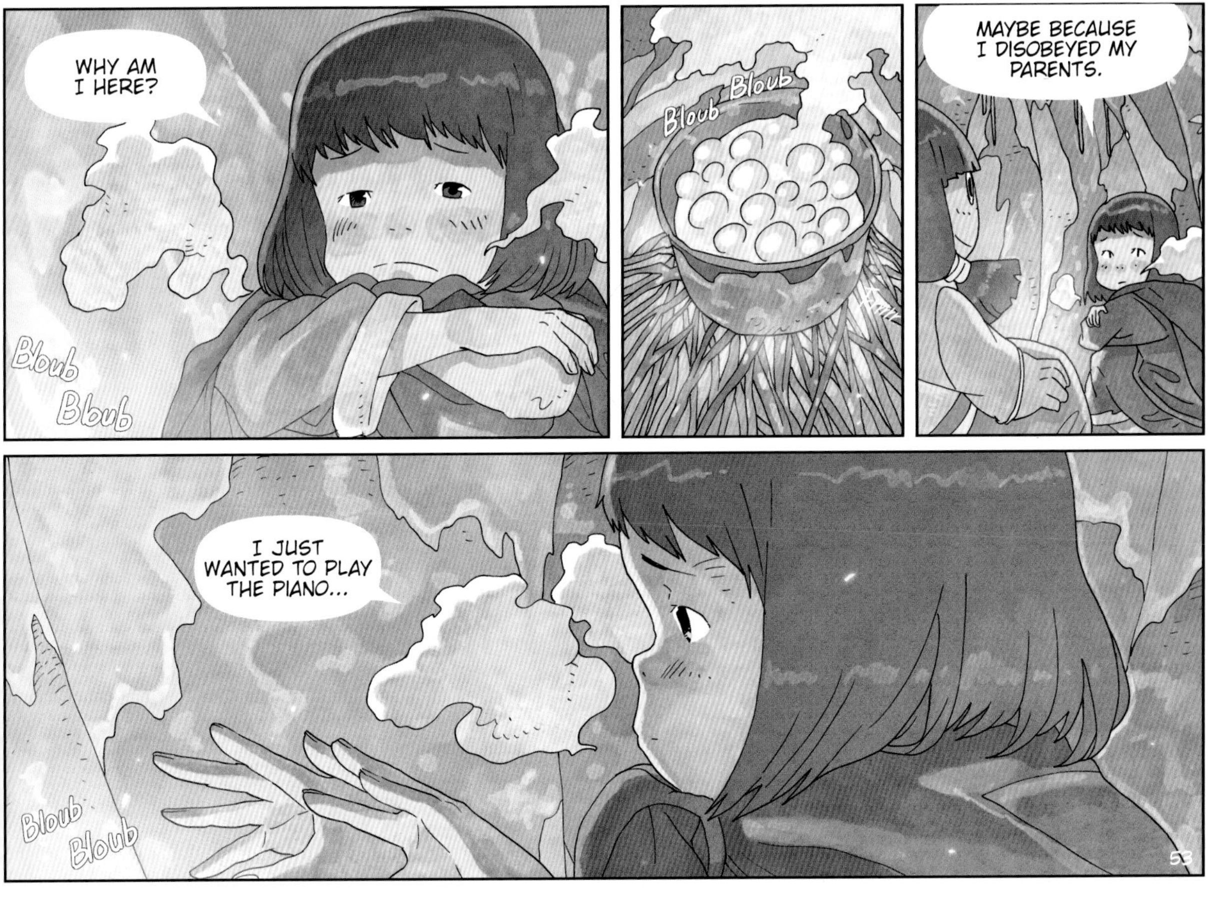
WHY AM I HERE?
Bloub
Bloub
Bloub
Bloub
MAYBE BECAUSE I DISOBEYED MY PARENTS.
I JUST WANTED TO PLAY THE PIANO...
Bloub
Bloub

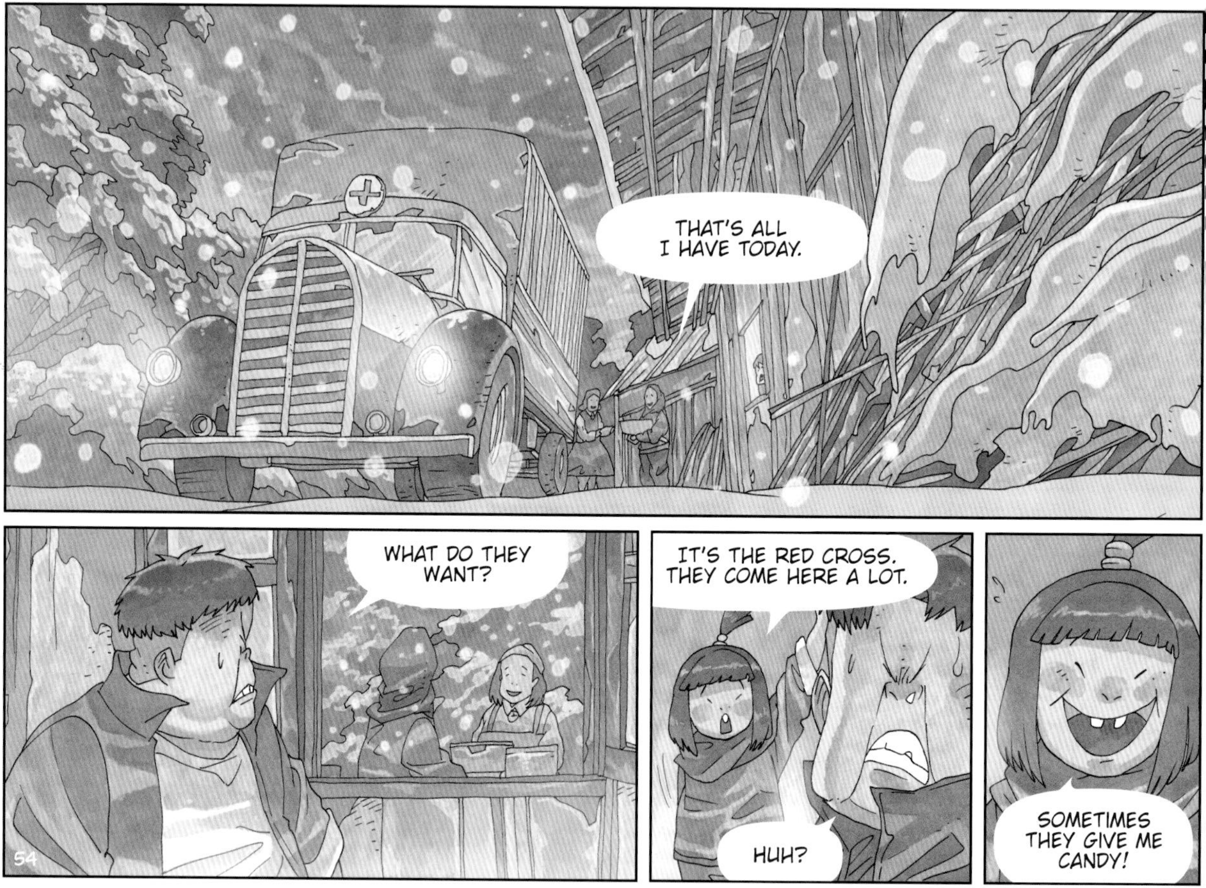
THAT'S ALL I HAVE TODAY.
WHAT DO THEY WANT?
IT'S THE RED CROSS. THEY COME HERE A LOT.
HUH?
SOMETIMES THEY GIVE ME CANDY!

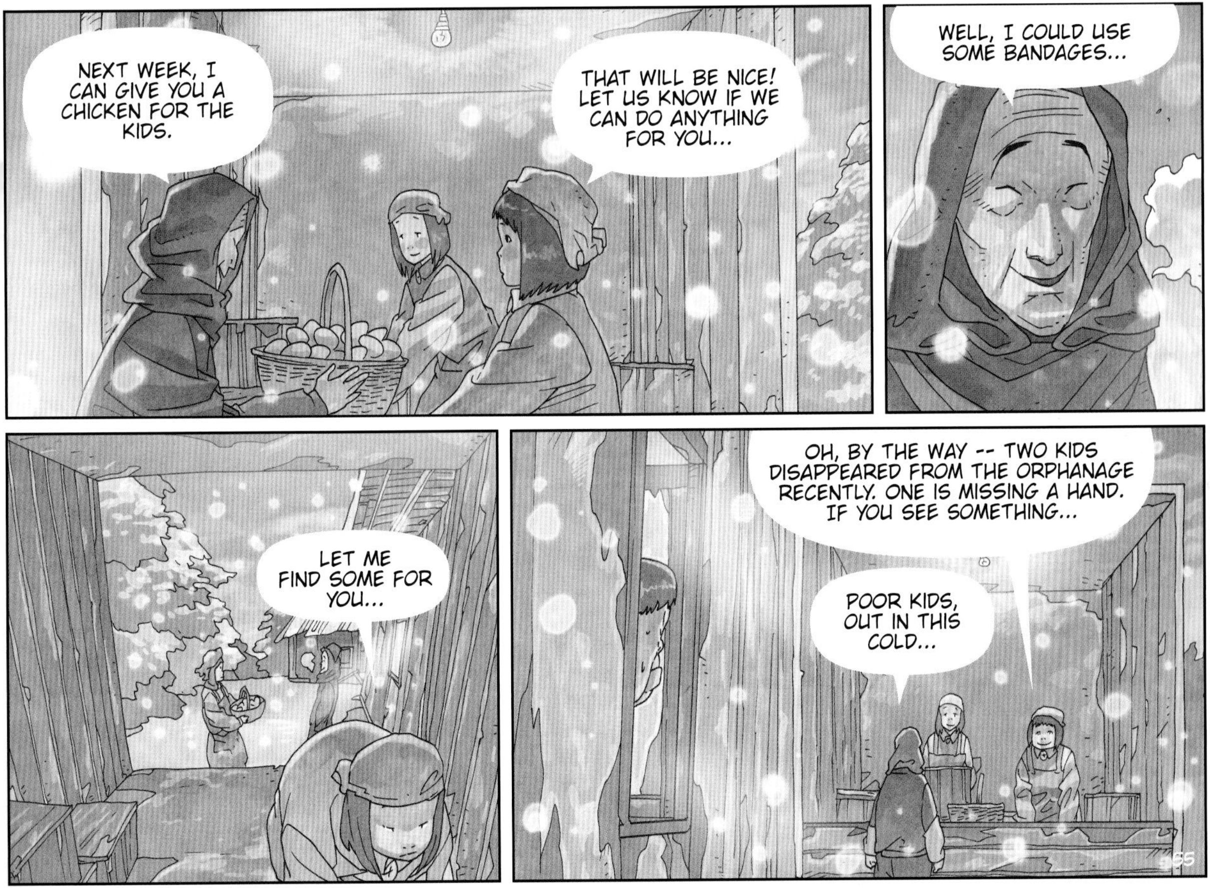
NEXT WEEK, I CAN GIVE YOU A CHICKEN FOR THE KIDS.
THAT WILL BE NICE! LET US KNOW IF WE CAN DO ANYTHING FOR YOU...
WELL, I COULD USE SOME BANDAGES...
LET ME FIND SOME FOR YOU...
OH, BY THE WAY -- TWO KIDS DISAPPEARED FROM THE ORPHANAGE RECENTLY. ONE IS MISSING A HAND. IF YOU SEE SOMETHING...
POOR KIDS, OUT IN THIS COLD...

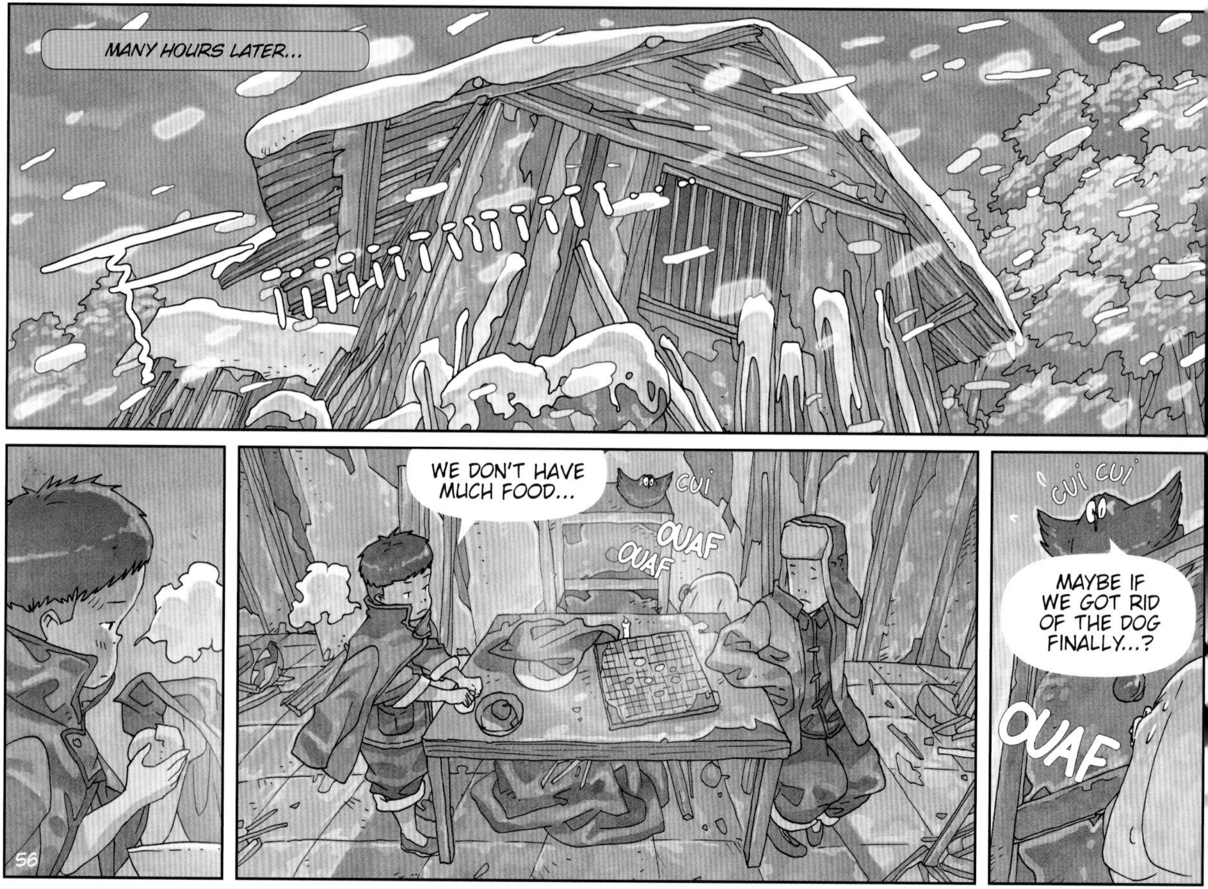

MANY HOURS LATER...
WE DON'T HAVE MUCH FOOD...
CUI
OUAF
OUAF
CUI CUI
MAYBE IF WE GOT RID OF THE DOG FINALLY...?
OUAF

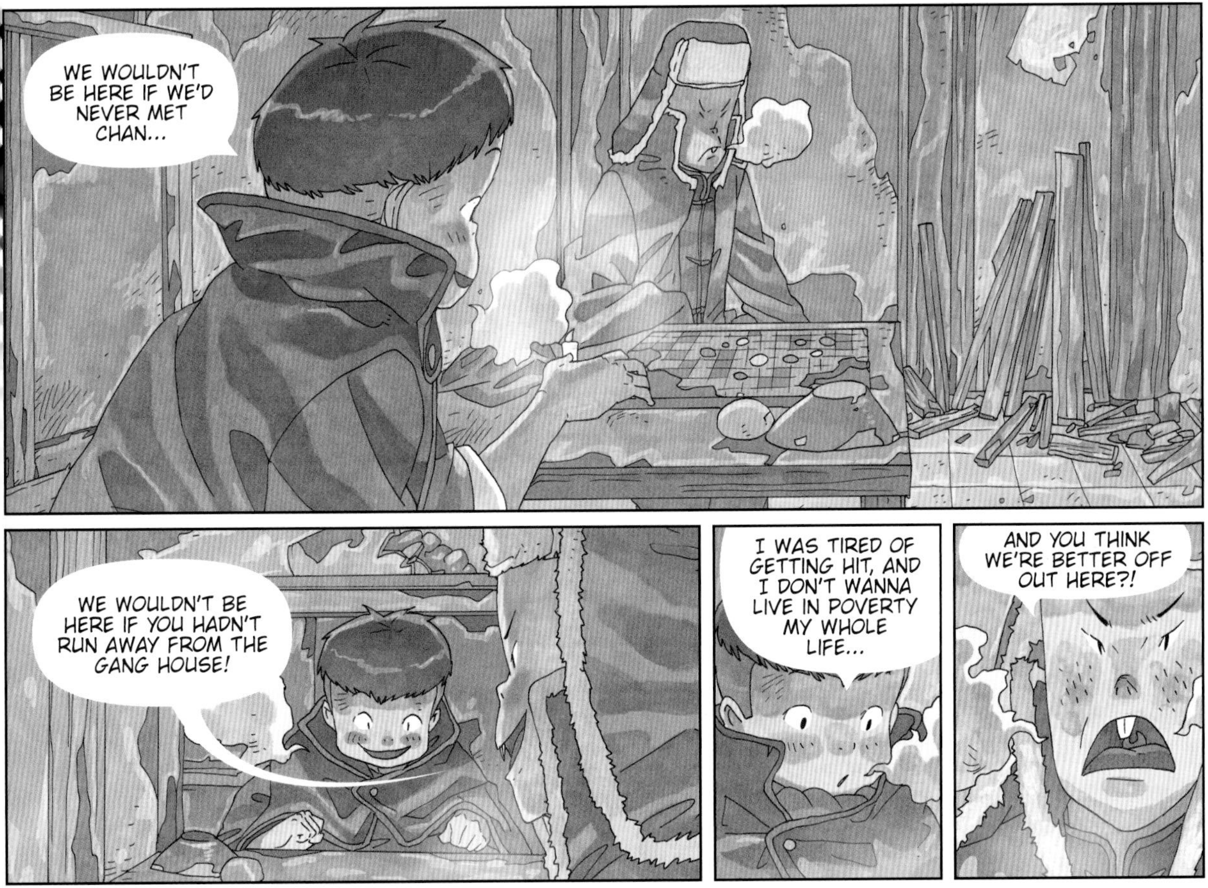
WE WOULDN'T BE HERE IF WE'D NEVER MET CHAN...
WE WOULDN'T BE HERE IF YOU HADN'T RUN AWAY FROM THE GANG HOUSE!
I WAS TIRED OF GETTING HIT, AND I DON'T WANNA LIVE IN POVERTY MY WHOLE LIFE...
AND YOU THINK WE'RE BETTER OFF OUT HERE?!

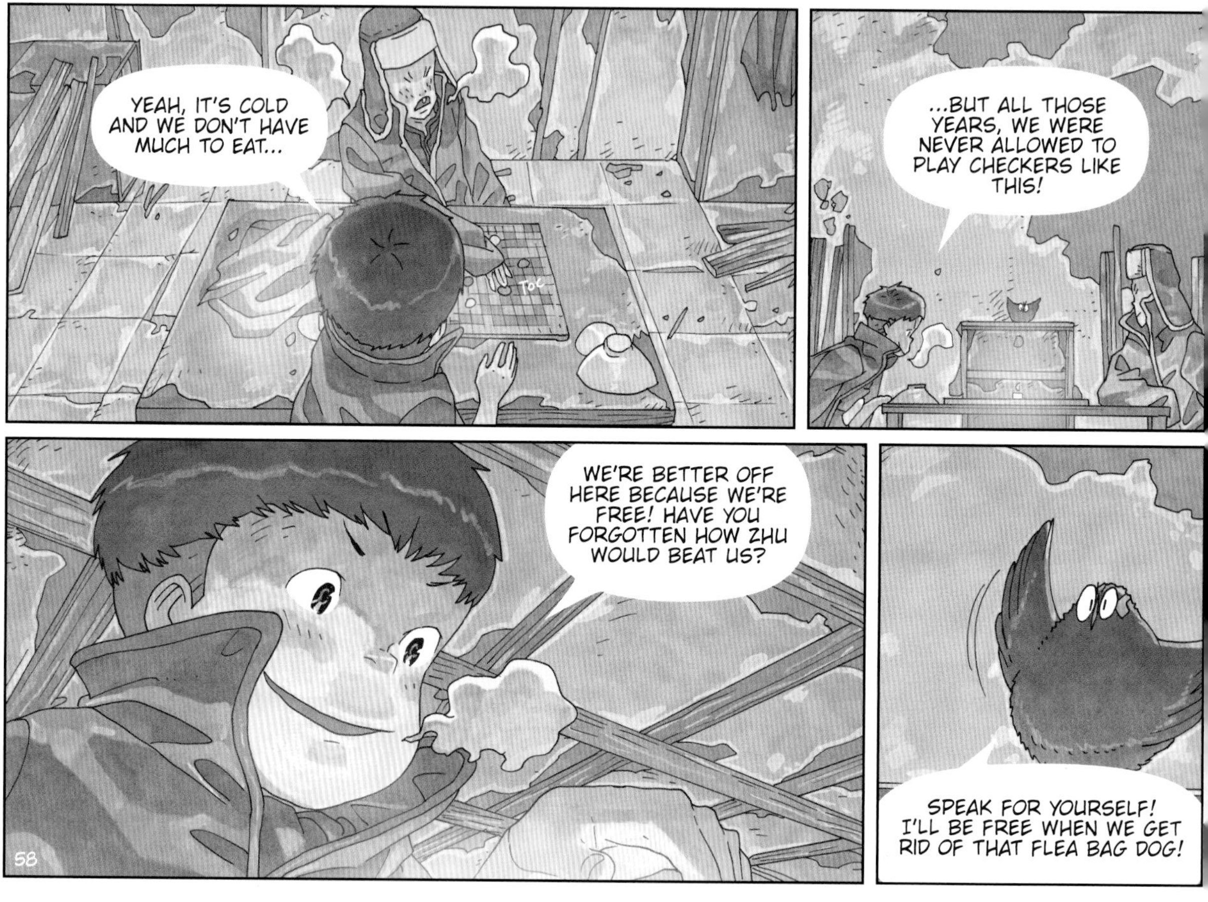
YEAH, IT'S COLD AND WE DON'T HAVE MUCH TO EAT...
TOC
...BUT ALL THOSE YEARS, WE WERE NEVER ALLOWED TO PLAY CHECKERS LIKE THIS!
WE'RE BETTER OFF HERE BECAUSE WE'RE FREE! HAVE YOU FORGOTTEN HOW ZHU WOULD BEAT US?
SPEAK FOR YOURSELF! I'LL BE FREE WHEN WE GET RID OF THAT FLEA BAG DOG!

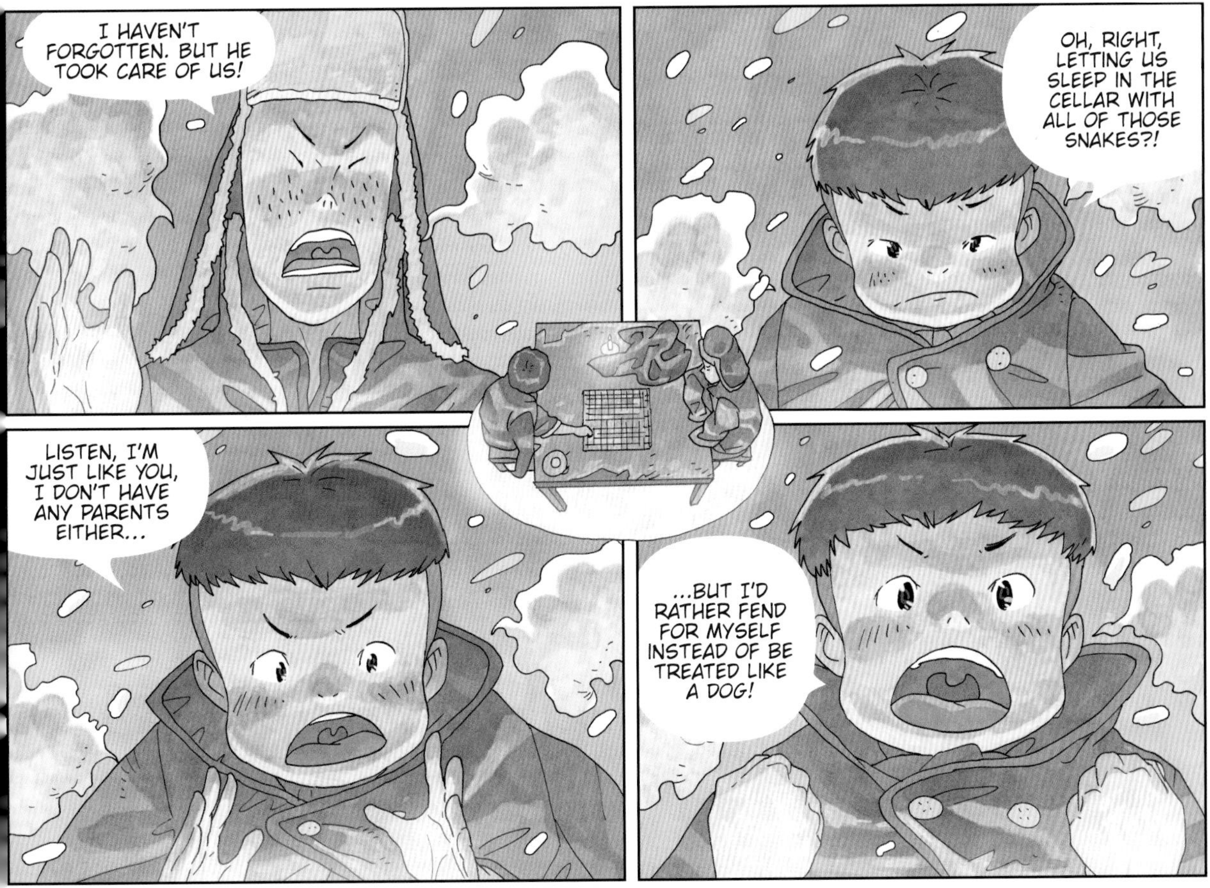
I HAVEN'T FORGOTTEN. BUT HE TOOK CARE OF US!
OH, RIGHT, LETTING US SLEEP IN THE CELLAR WITH ALL OF THOSE SNAKES?!
LISTEN, I'M JUST LIKE YOU, I DON'T HAVE ANY PARENTS EITHER...
...BUT I'D RATHER FEND FOR MYSELF INSTEAD OF BE TREATED LIKE A DOG!

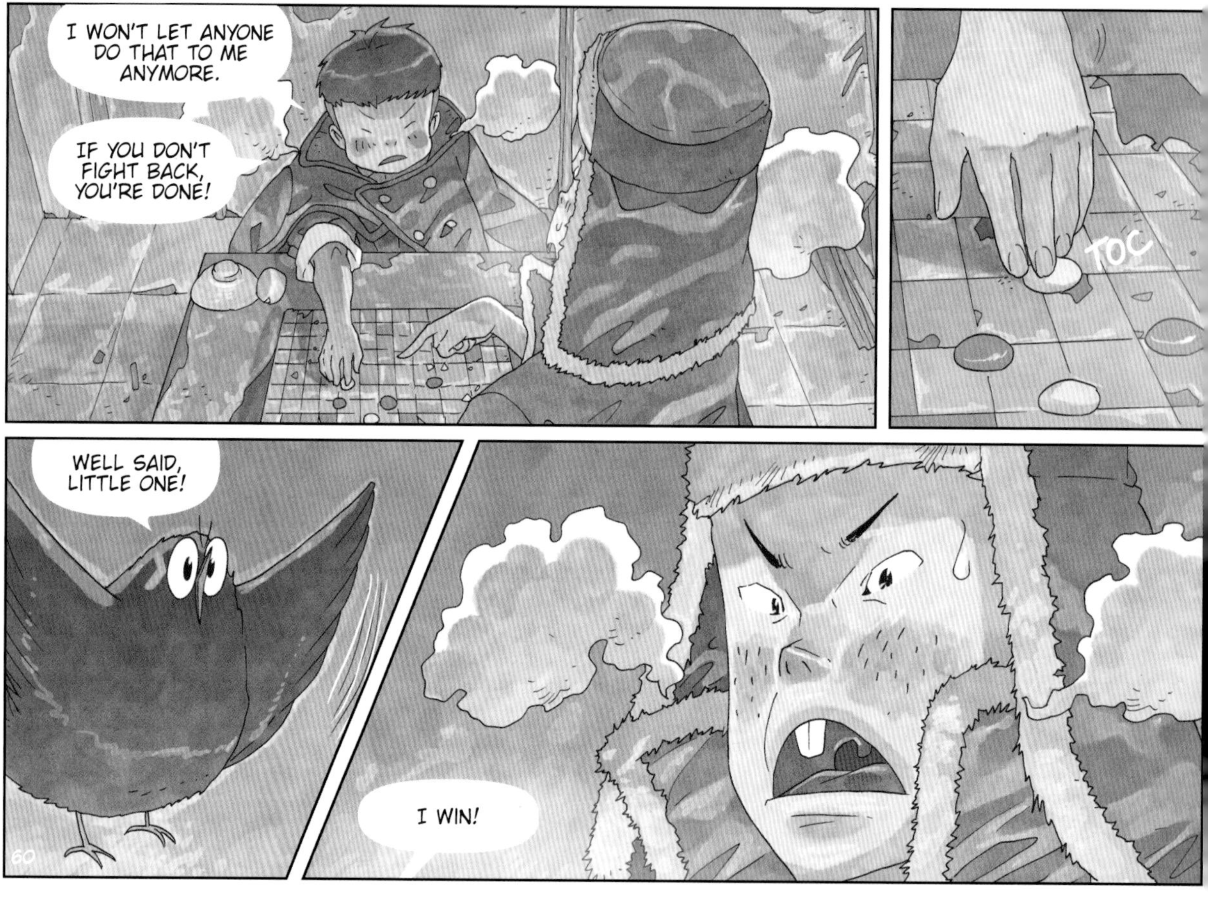
I WON'T LET ANYONE DO THAT TO ME ANYMORE.
IF YOU DON'T FIGHT BACK, YOU'RE DONE!
TOC
WELL SAID, LITTLE ONE!
I WIN!

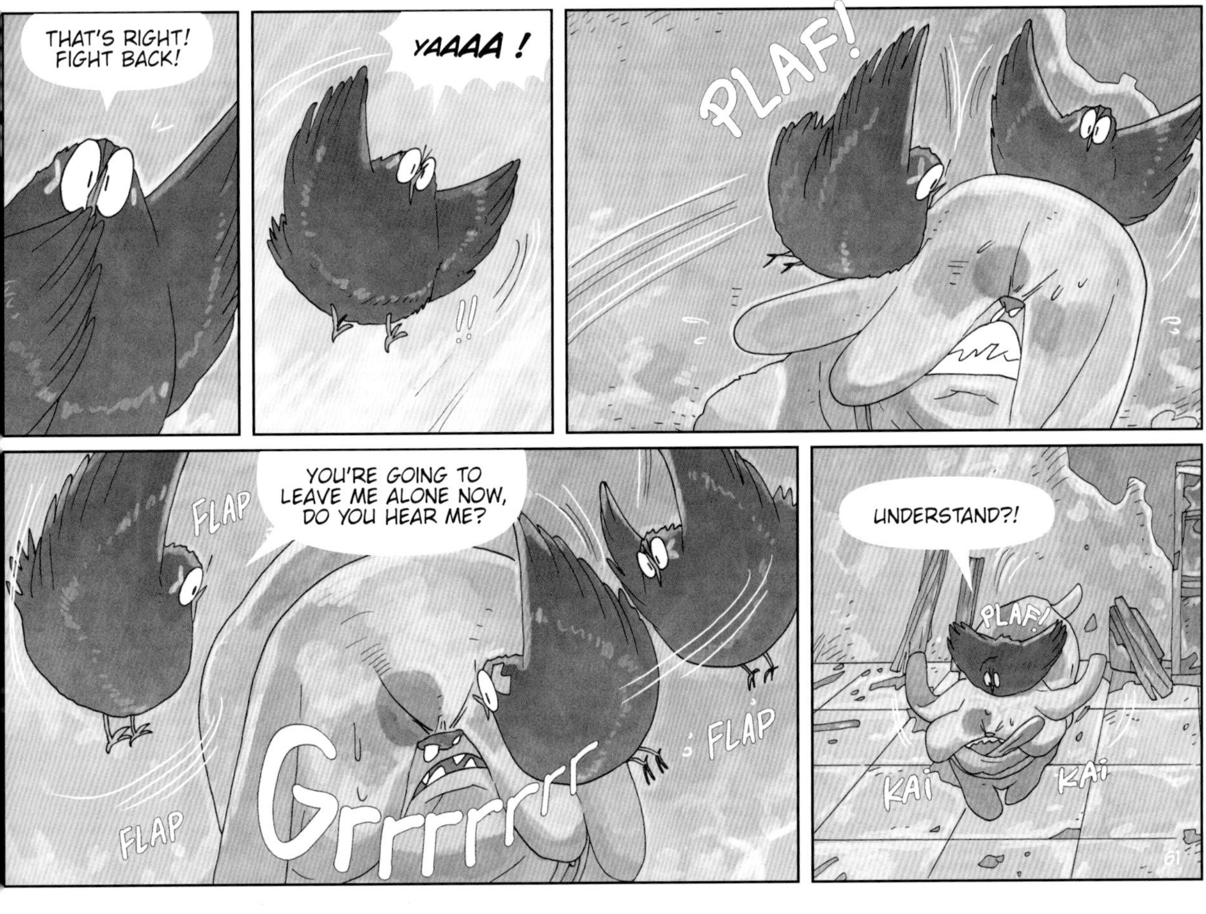
THAT'S RIGHT! FIGHT BACK!
YAAAA !
!!
PLAF!
FLAP
YOU'RE GOING TO LEAVE ME ALONE NOW, DO YOU HEAR ME?
FLAP
FLAP
Grrrrrrr
UNDERSTAND?!
PLAF!
KAI
KAI

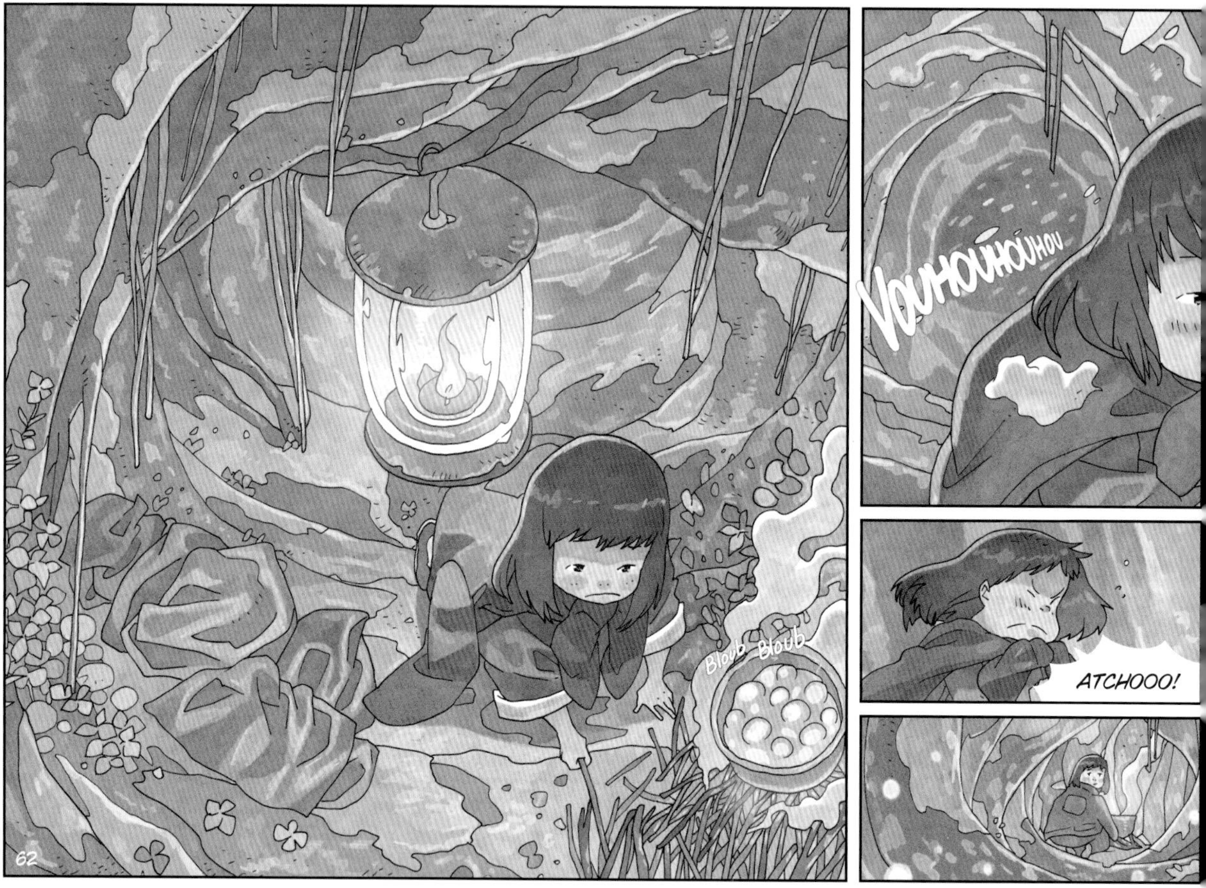
Bloub Bloub
VOUHOUHOUHOU
ATCHOOO!

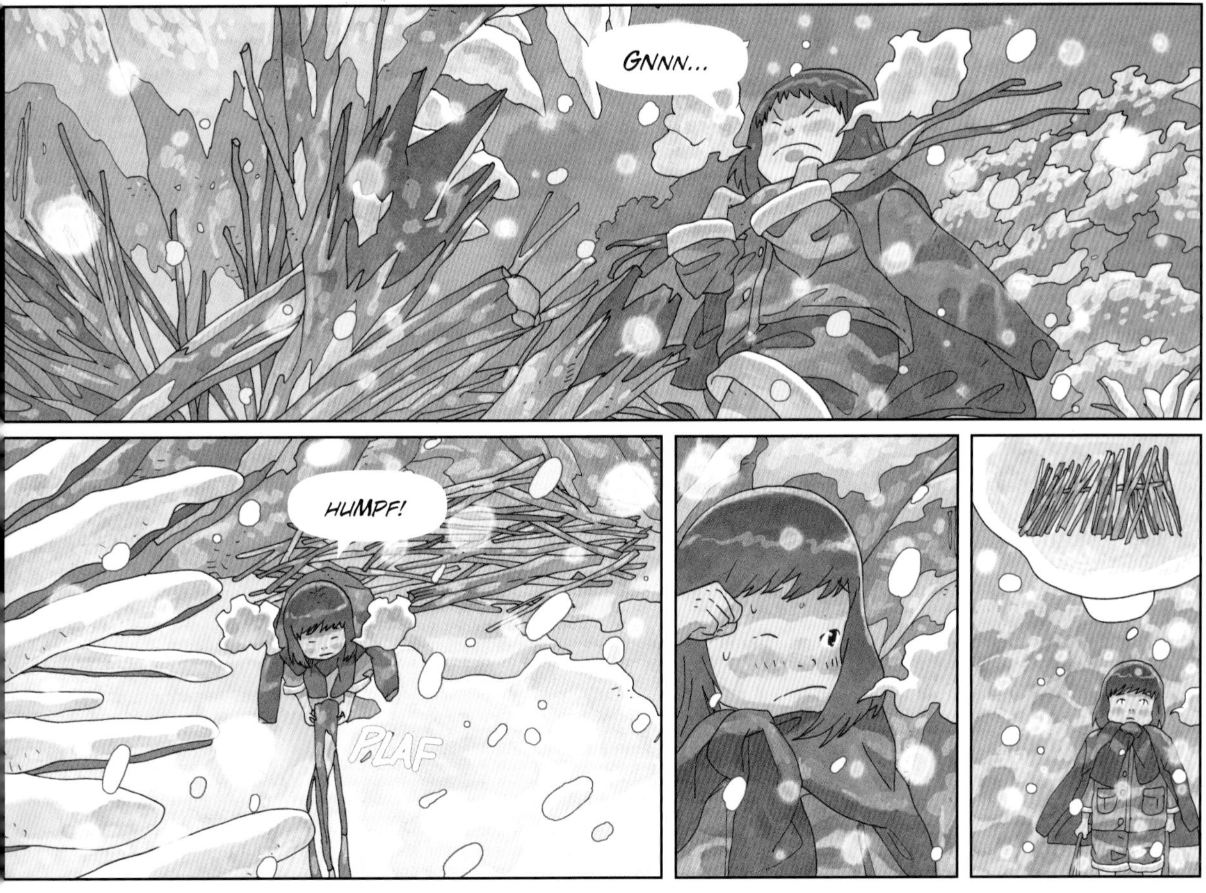
GNNN...
HUMPF!
PLAF

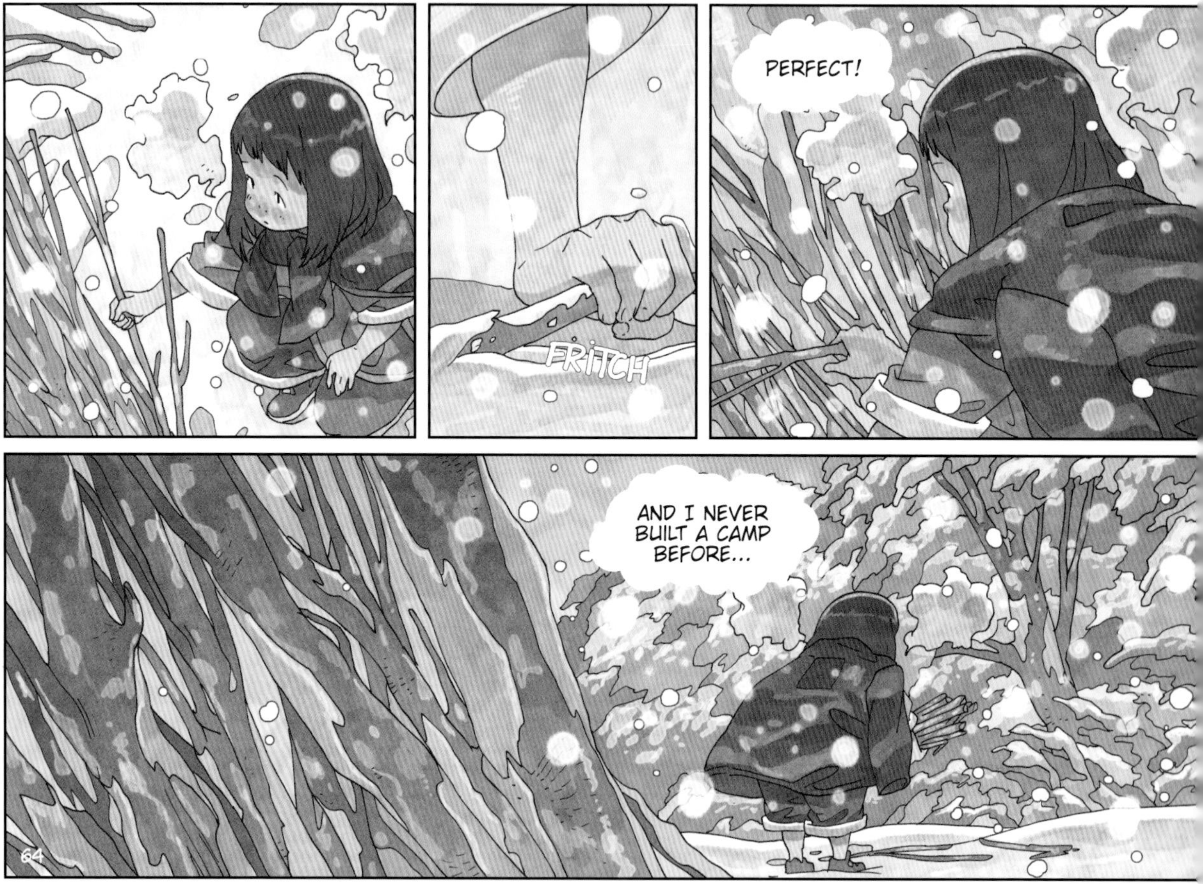
FRITCH
PERFECT!
AND I NEVER BUILT A CAMP BEFORE...

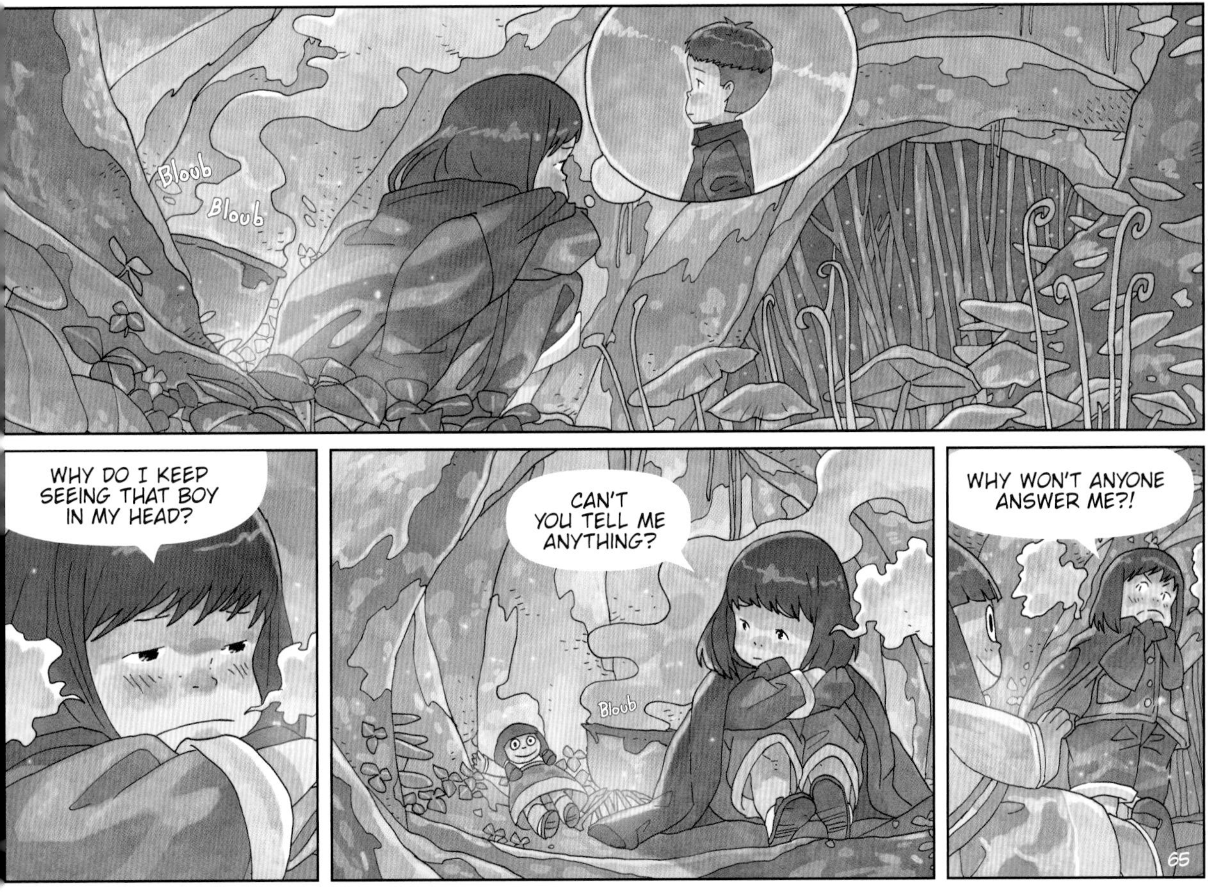
Bloub
Bloub
WHY DO I KEEP SEEING THAT BOY IN MY HEAD?
CAN'T YOU TELL ME ANYTHING?
Bloub
WHY WON'T ANYONE ANSWER ME?!

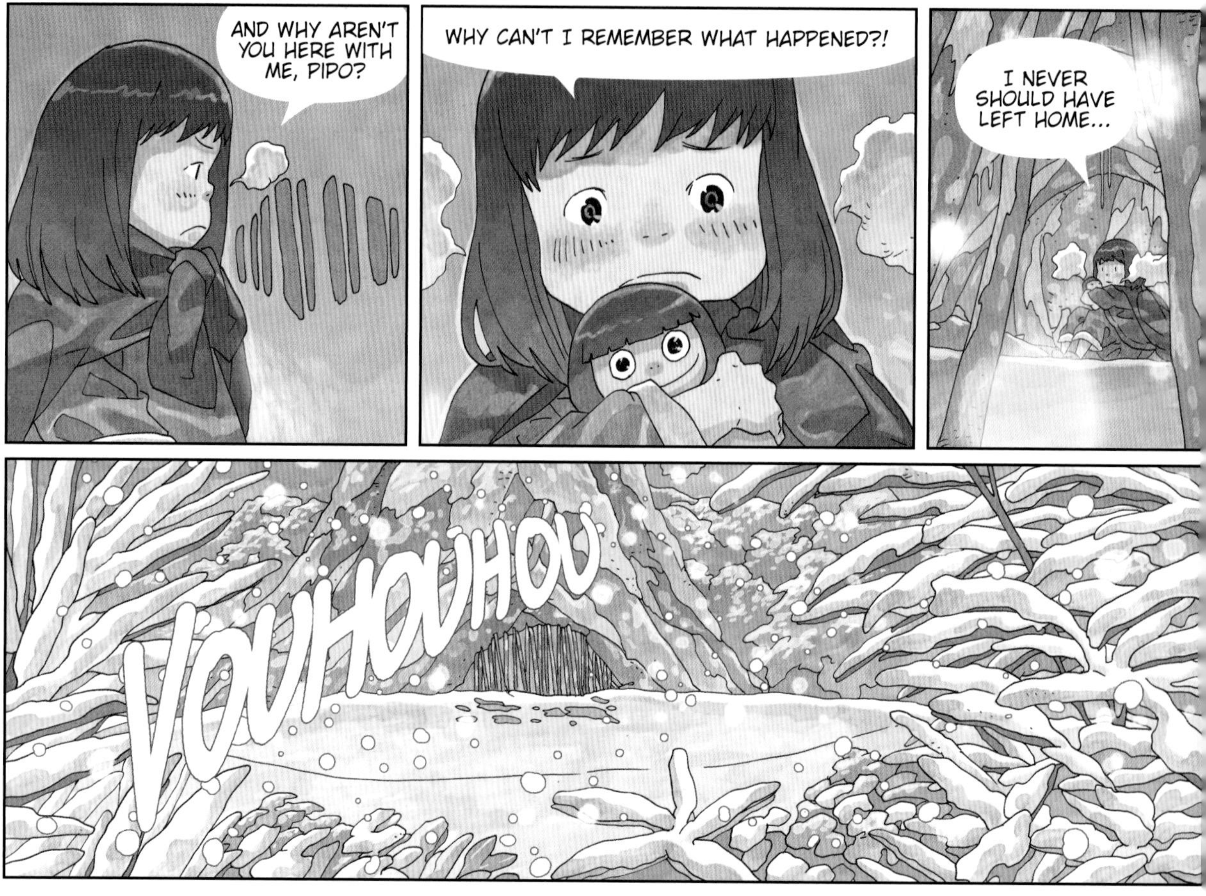
AND WHY AREN'T YOU HERE WITH ME, PIPO?
WHY CAN'T I REMEMBER WHAT HAPPENED?!
I NEVER SHOULD HAVE LEFT HOME...
VOUHOUHOU

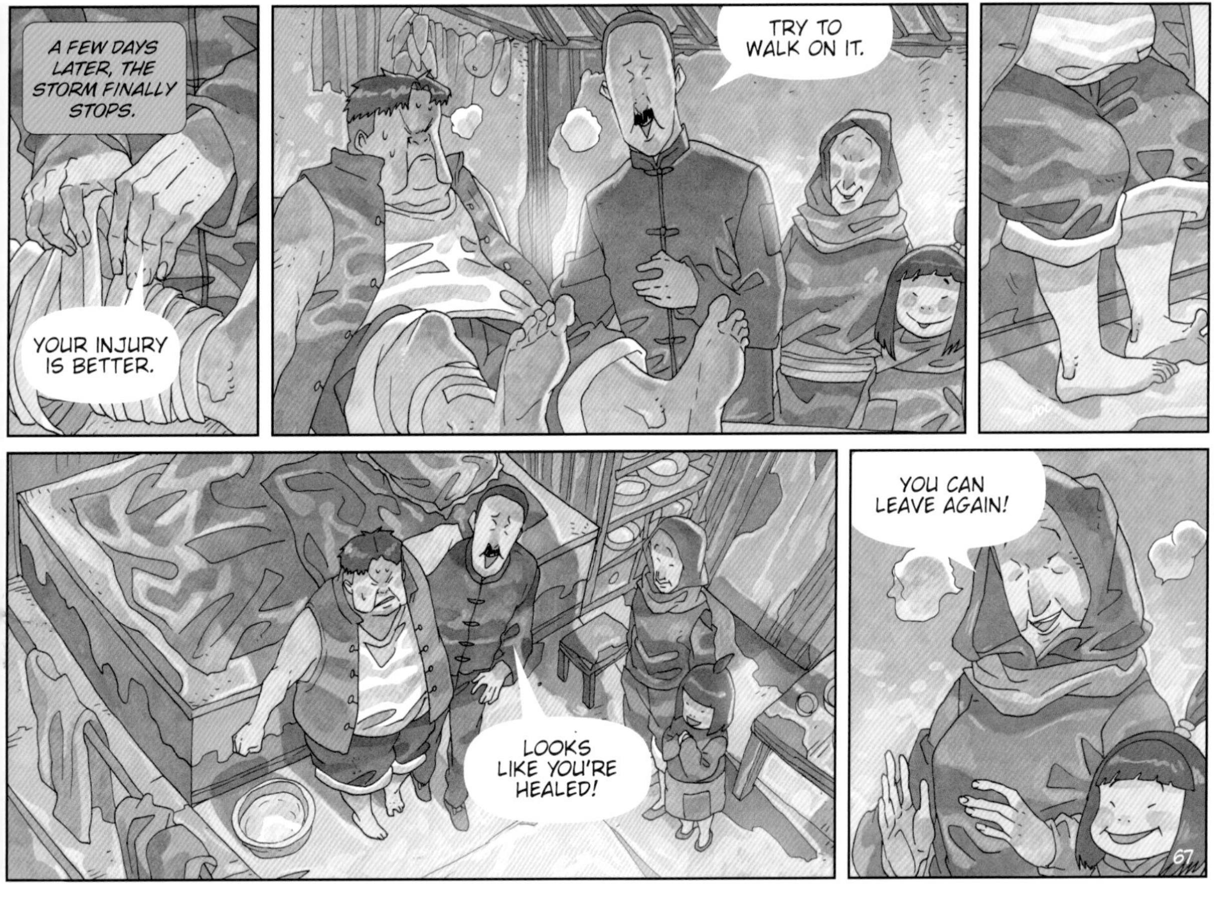
A FEW DAYS LATER, THE STORM FINALLY STOPS.
YOUR INJURY IS BETTER.
TRY TO WALK ON IT.
LOOKS LIKE YOU'RE HEALED!
YOU CAN LEAVE AGAIN!

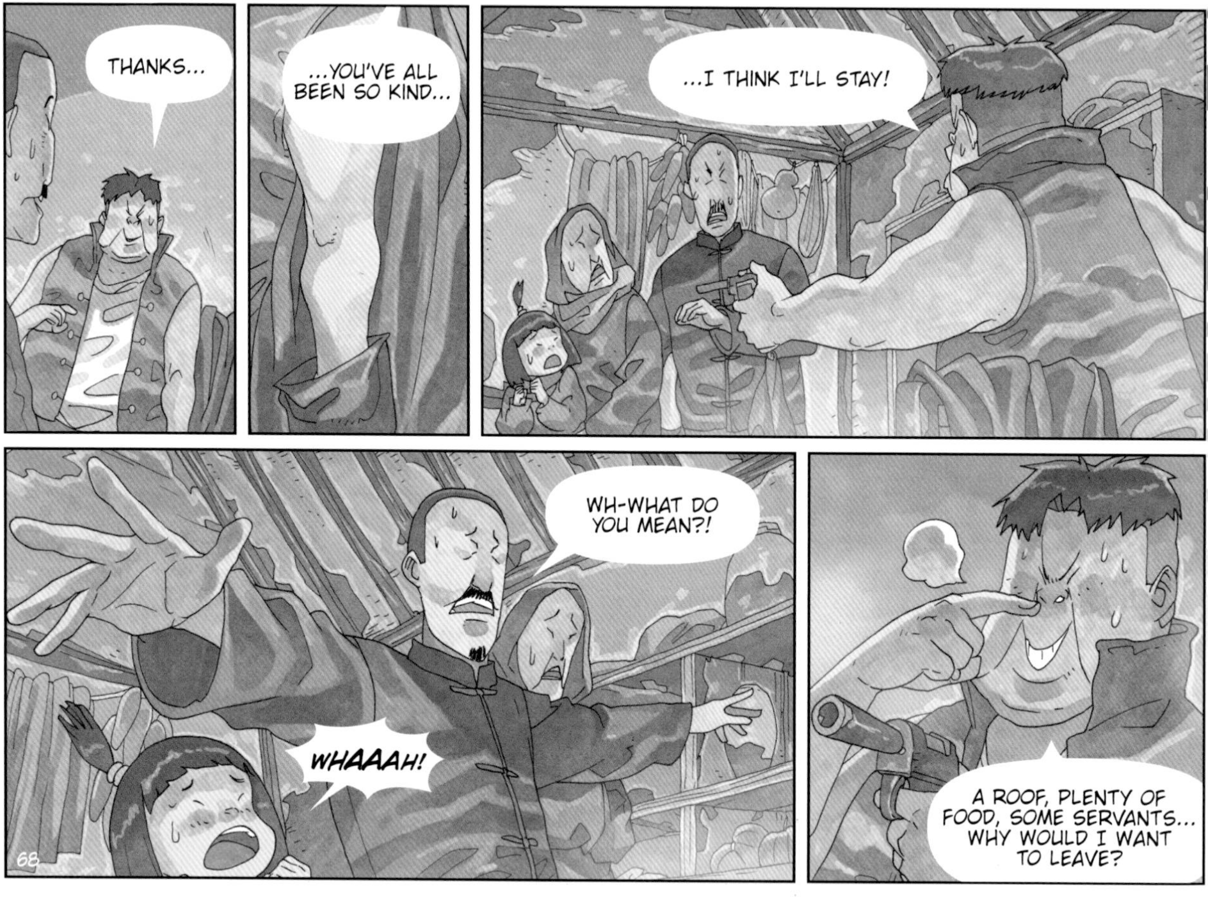
THANKS...
...YOU'VE ALL BEEN SO KIND...
...I THINK I'LL STAY!
WH-WHAT DO YOU MEAN?!
WHAAAH!
A ROOF, PLENTY OF FOOD, SOME SERVANTS... WHY WOULD I WANT TO LEAVE?

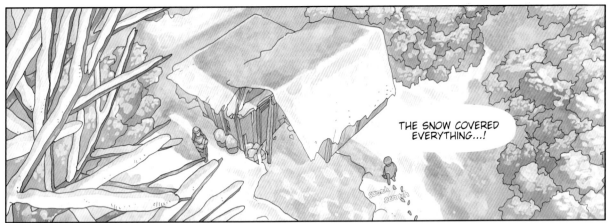

THE SNOW COVERED EVERYTHING...!

NOT A TRACE OF YAYA...

MAYBE THIS IS THE WRONG HOUSE...?

BUT... OH NO!

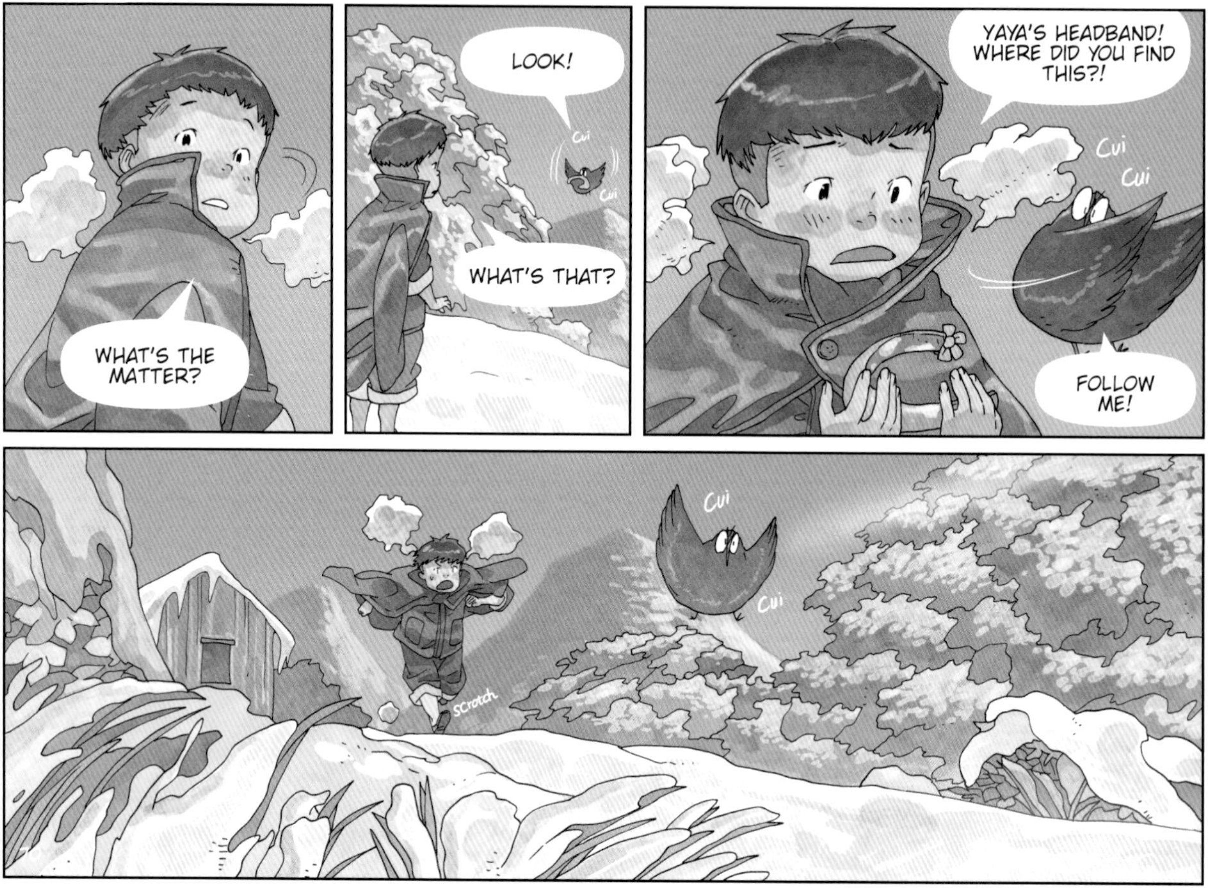

WHAT'S THE MATTER?
LOOK!
Cui
Cui
WHAT'S THAT?
YAYA'S HEADBAND! WHERE DID YOU FIND THIS?!
Cui
Cui
FOLLOW ME!
Cui
Cui
SCROTCH

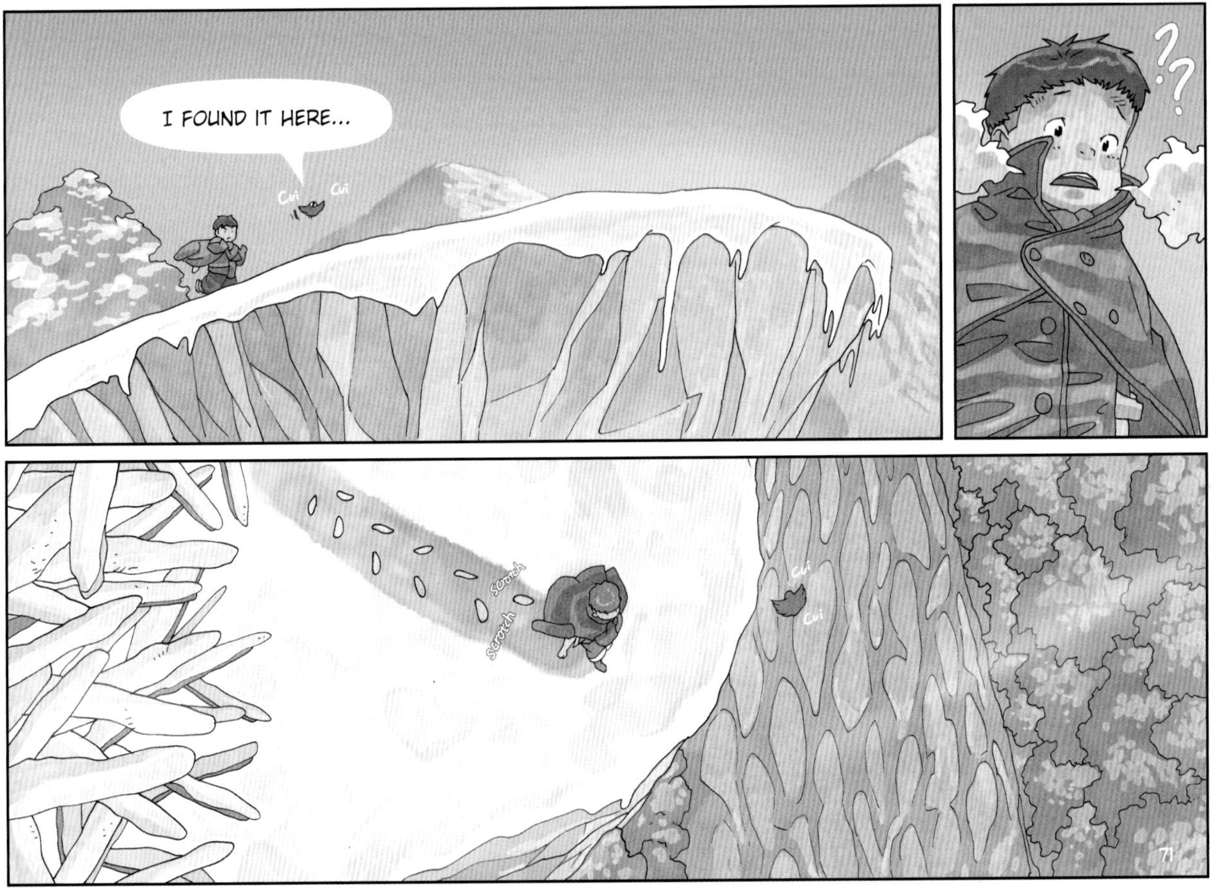
I FOUND IT HERE...
Cui
Cui
??
Scrotch
Scrotch
Cui
Cui

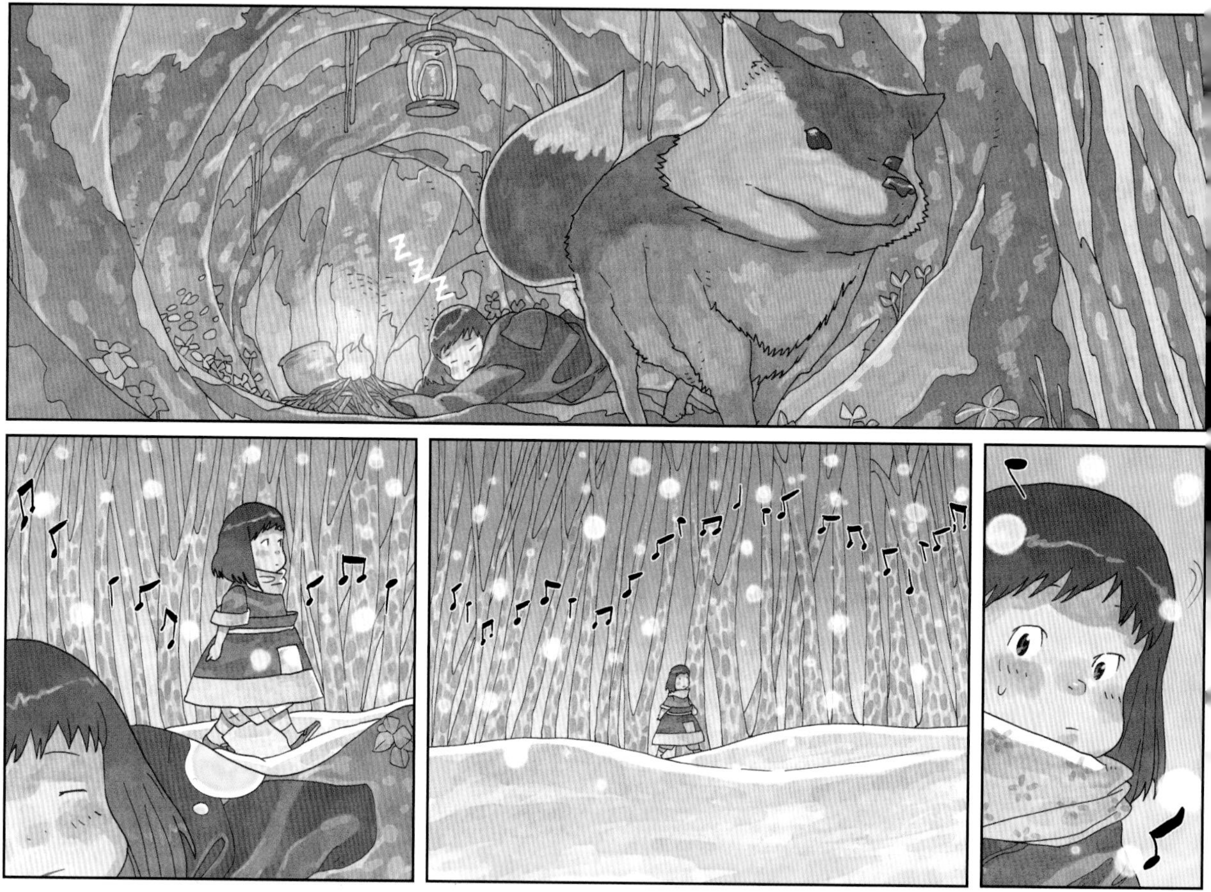
ZZZ

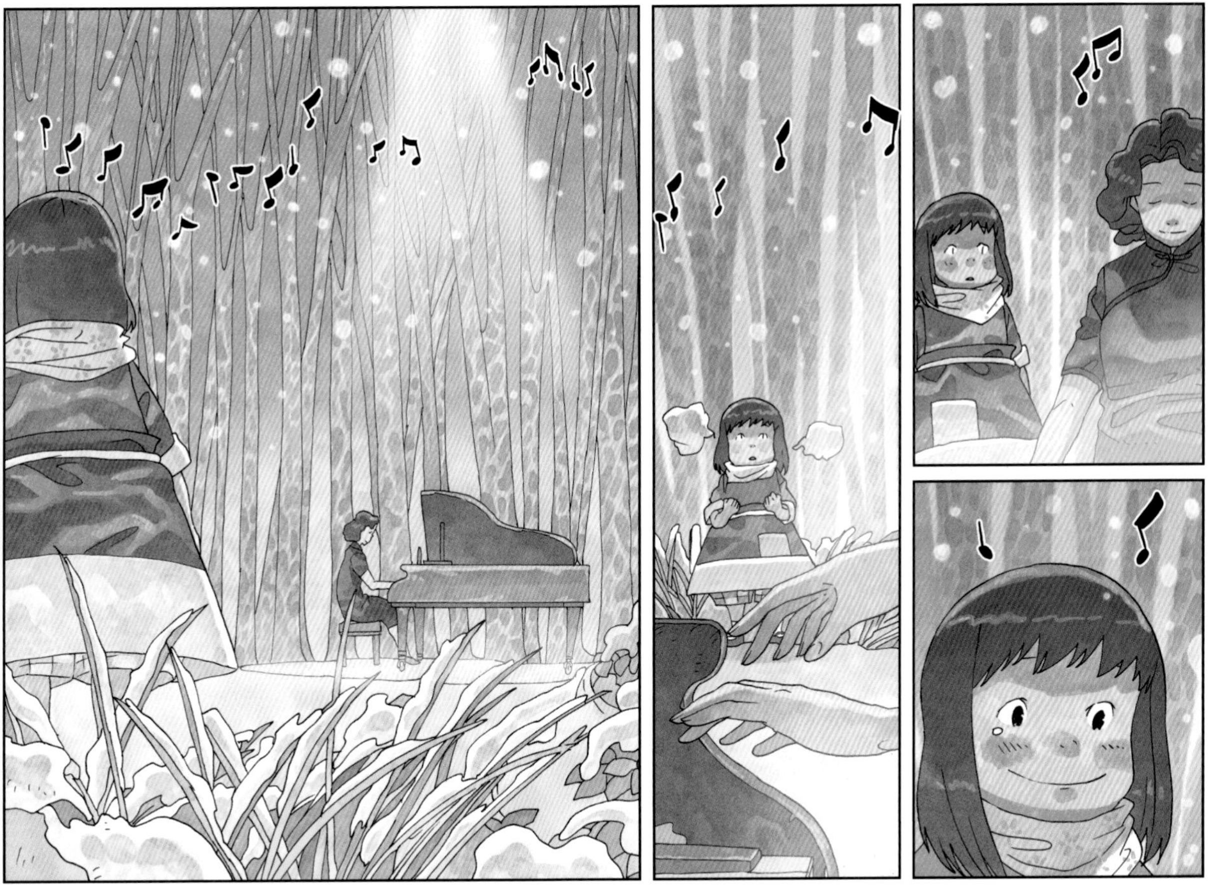

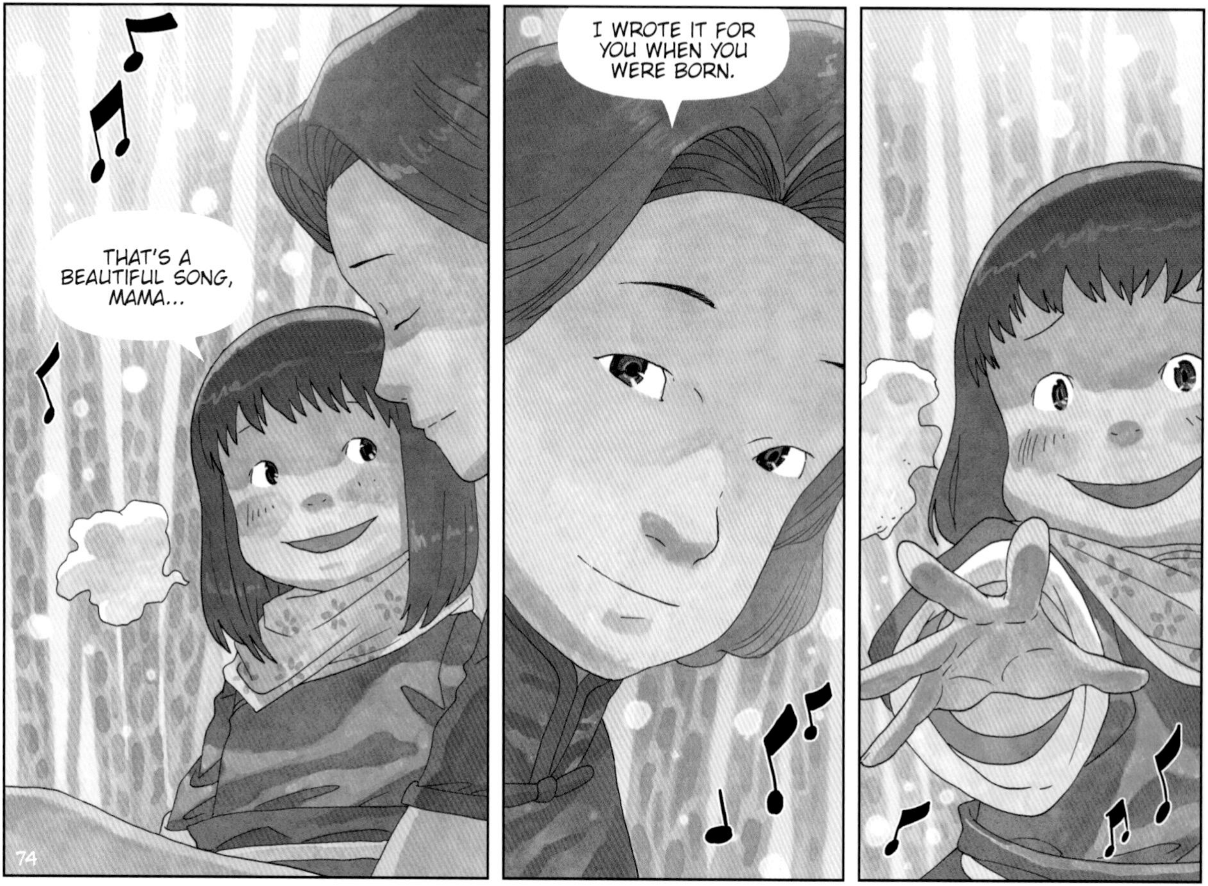

THAT'S A BEAUTIFUL SONG, MAMA...
I WROTE IT FOR YOU WHEN YOU WERE BORN.

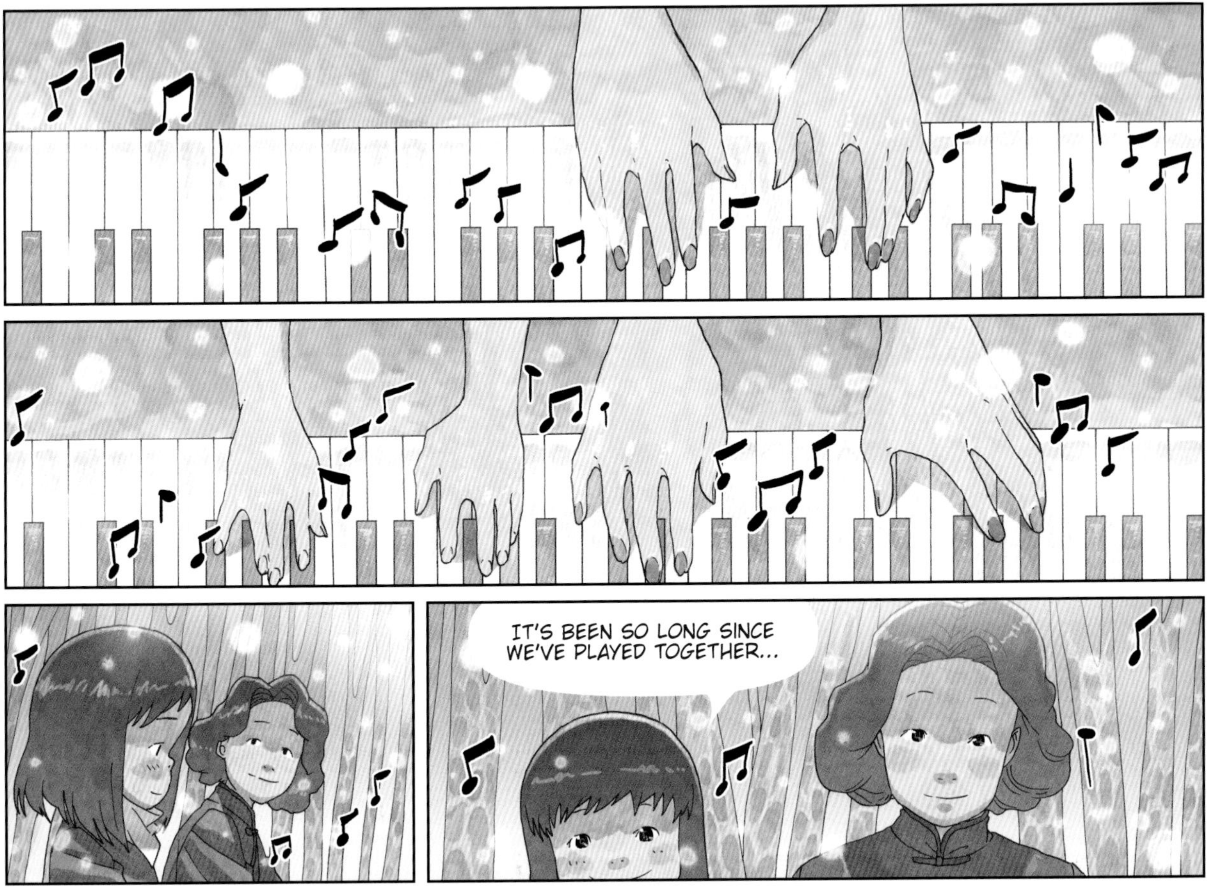
IT'S BEEN SO LONG SINCE WE'VE PLAYED TOGETHER...

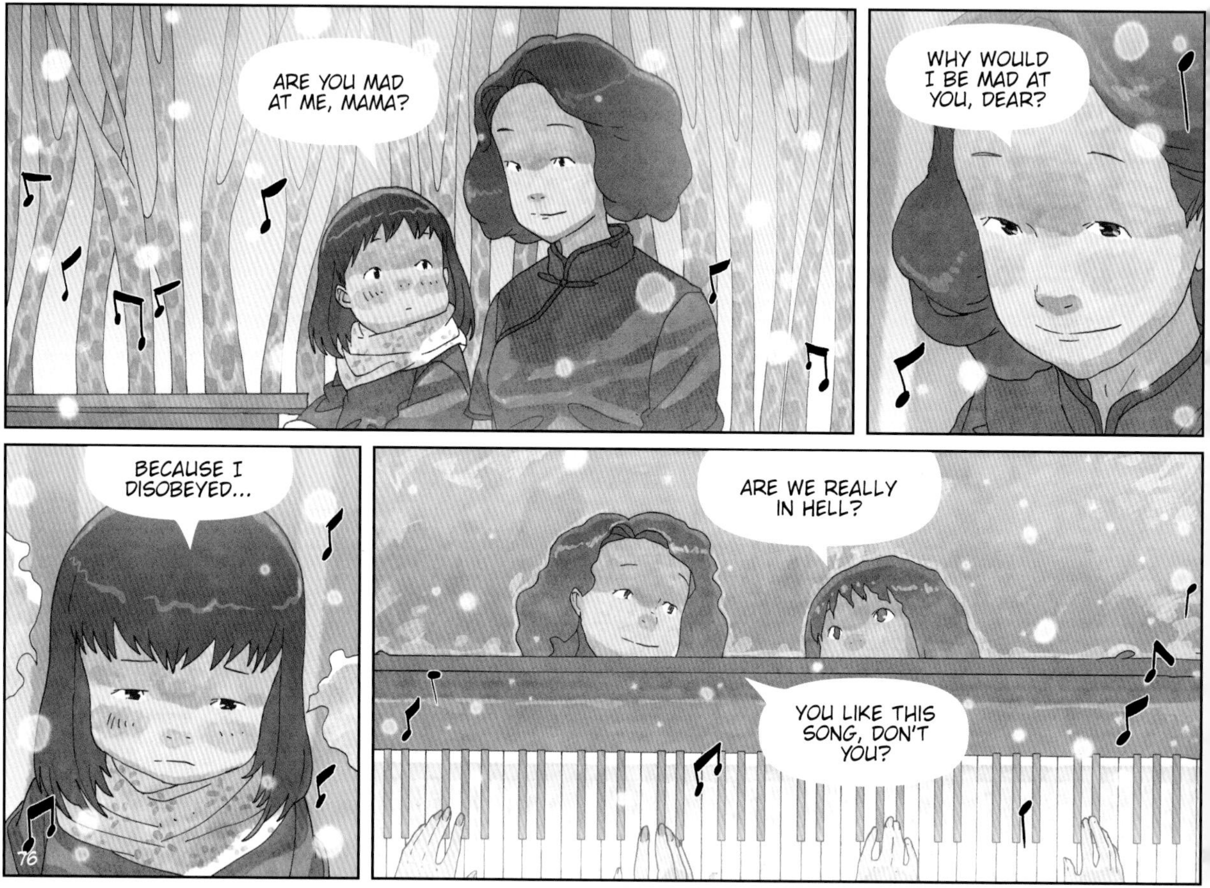
ARE YOU MAD AT ME, MAMA?
WHY WOULD I BE MAD AT YOU, DEAR?
BECAUSE I DISOBEYED...
ARE WE REALLY IN HELL?
YOU LIKE THIS SONG, DON'T YOU?

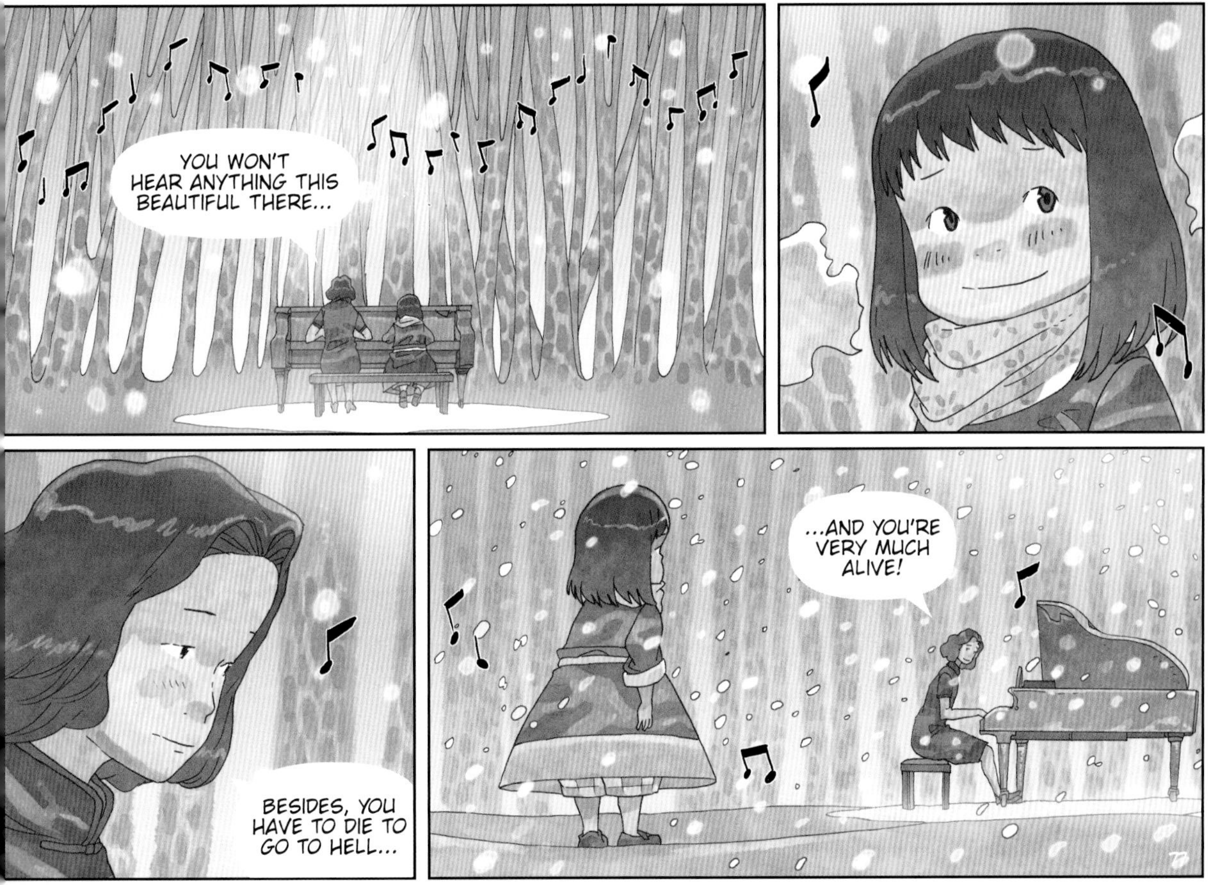

YOU WON'T HEAR ANYTHING THIS BEAUTIFUL THERE...
BESIDES, YOU HAVE TO DIE TO GO TO HELL...
...AND YOU'RE VERY MUCH ALIVE!

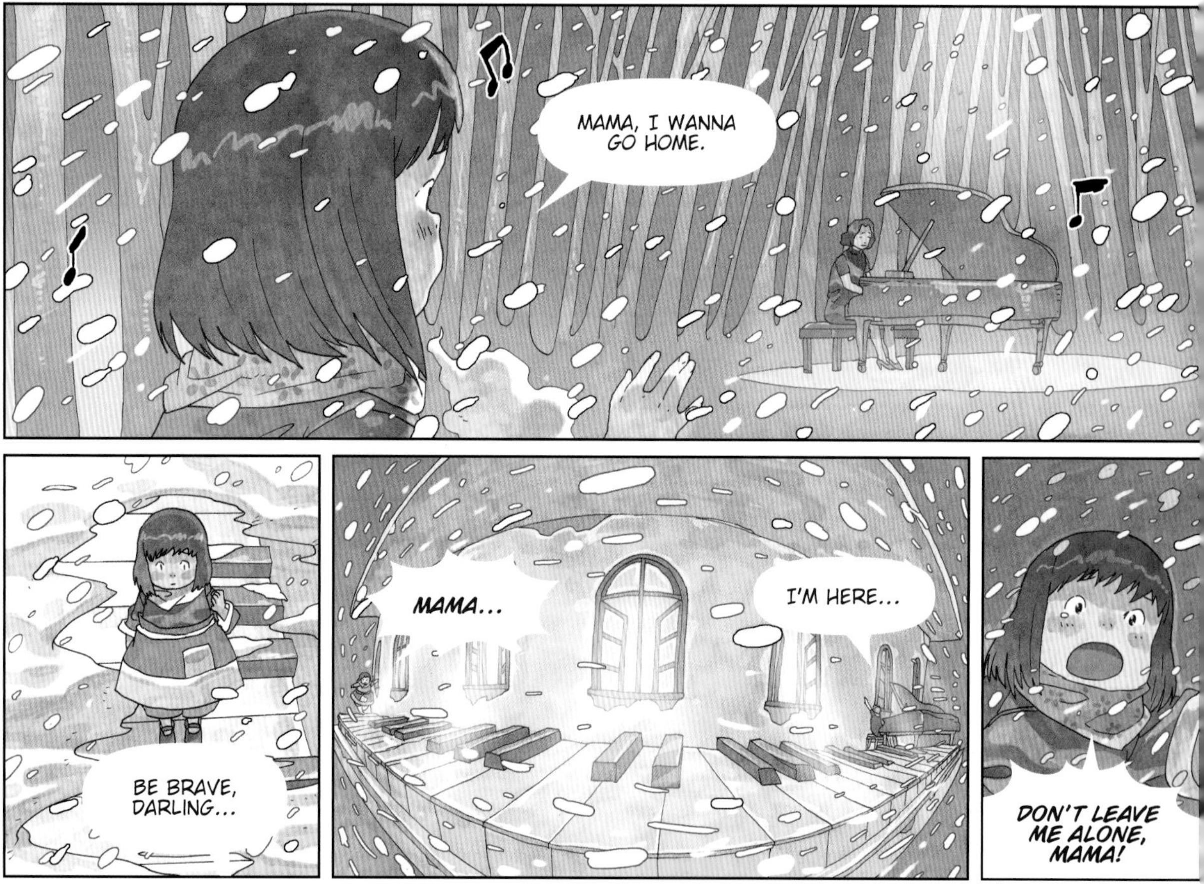
MAMA, I WANNA GO HOME.
BE BRAVE, DARLING...
MAMA...
I'M HERE...
DON'T LEAVE ME ALONE, MAMA!

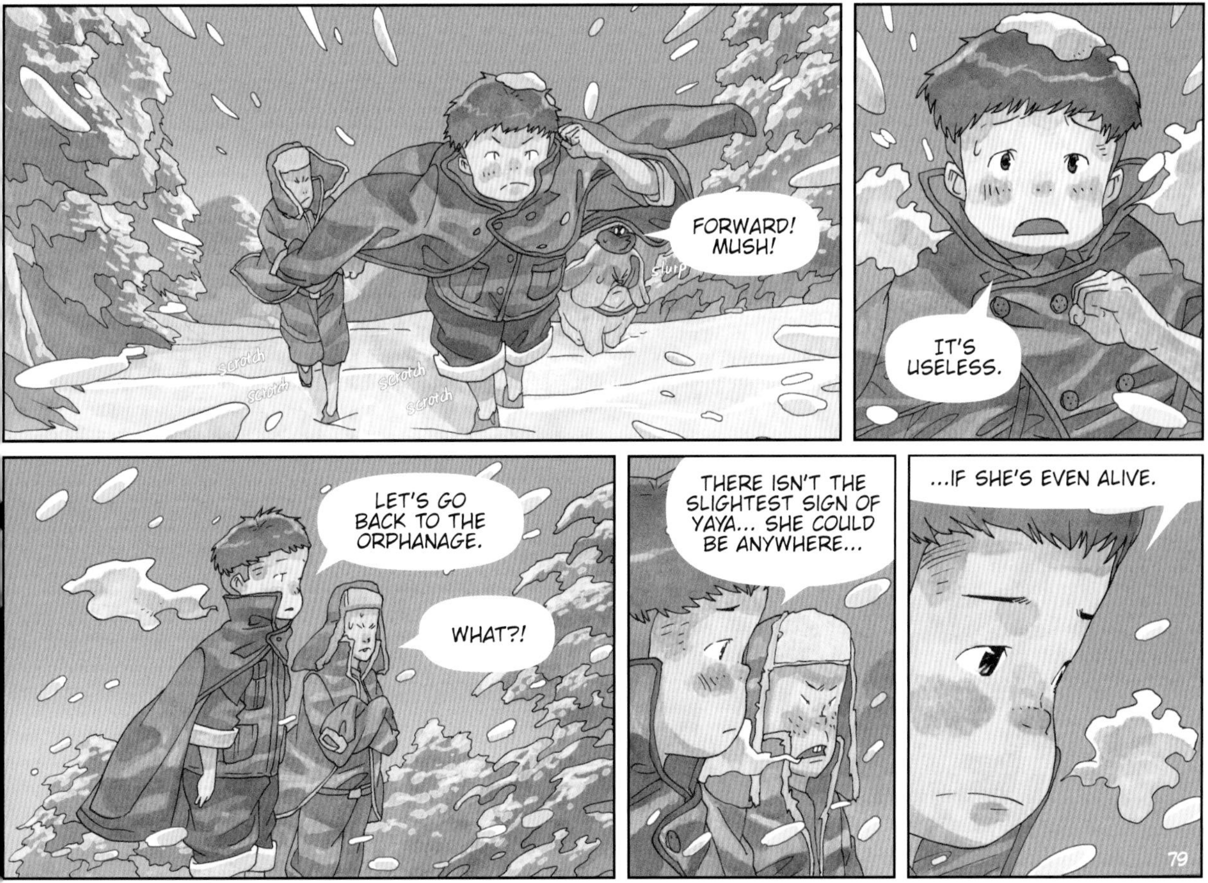

FORWARD! MUSH!
slurp
scrotch
scrotch
scrotch
scrotch
IT'S USELESS.
LET'S GO BACK TO THE ORPHANAGE.
WHAT?!
THERE ISN'T THE SLIGHTEST SIGN OF YAYA... SHE COULD BE ANYWHERE...
...IF SHE'S EVEN ALIVE.

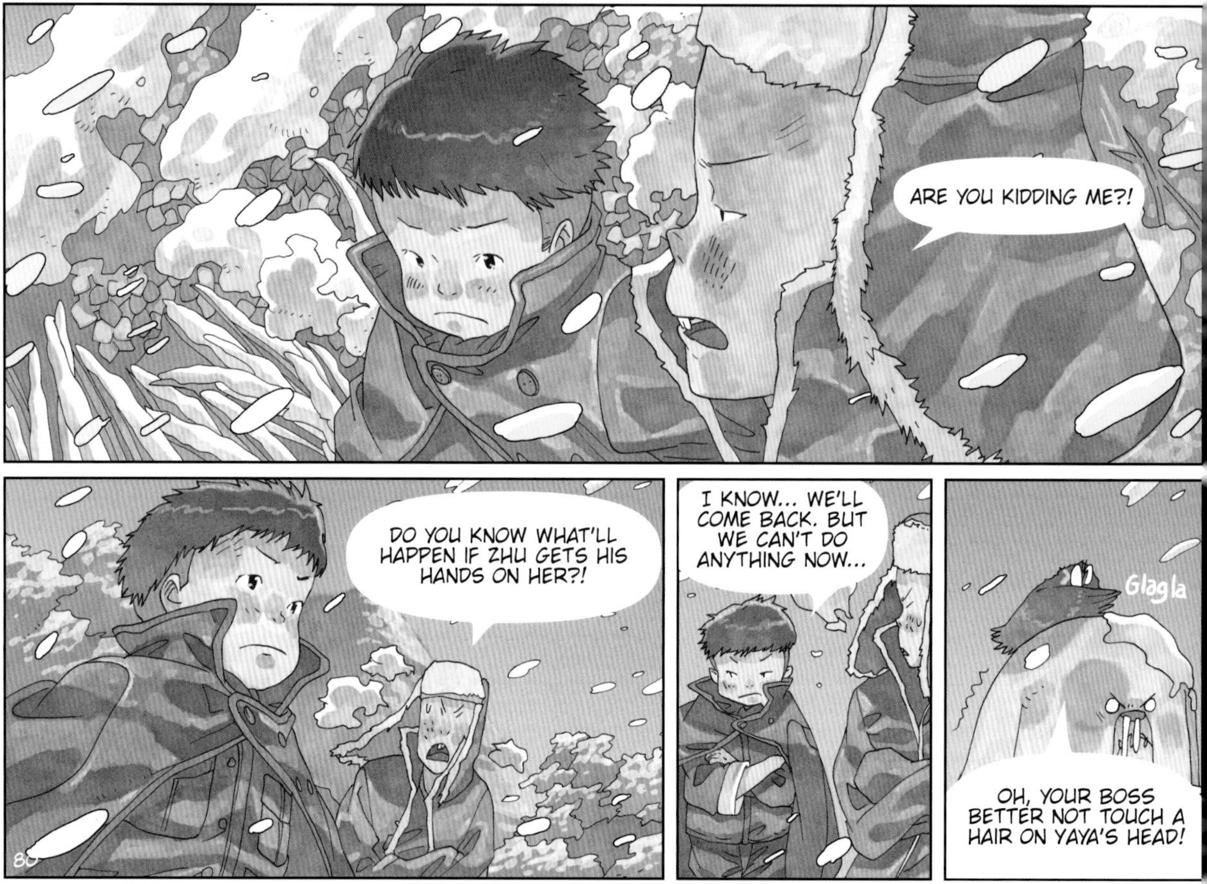

ARE YOU KIDDING ME?!
DO YOU KNOW WHAT'LL HAPPEN IF ZHU GETS HIS HANDS ON HER?!
I KNOW... WE'LL COME BACK. BUT WE CAN'T DO ANYTHING NOW...
Glagla
OH, YOUR BOSS BETTER NOT TOUCH A HAIR ON YAYA'S HEAD!

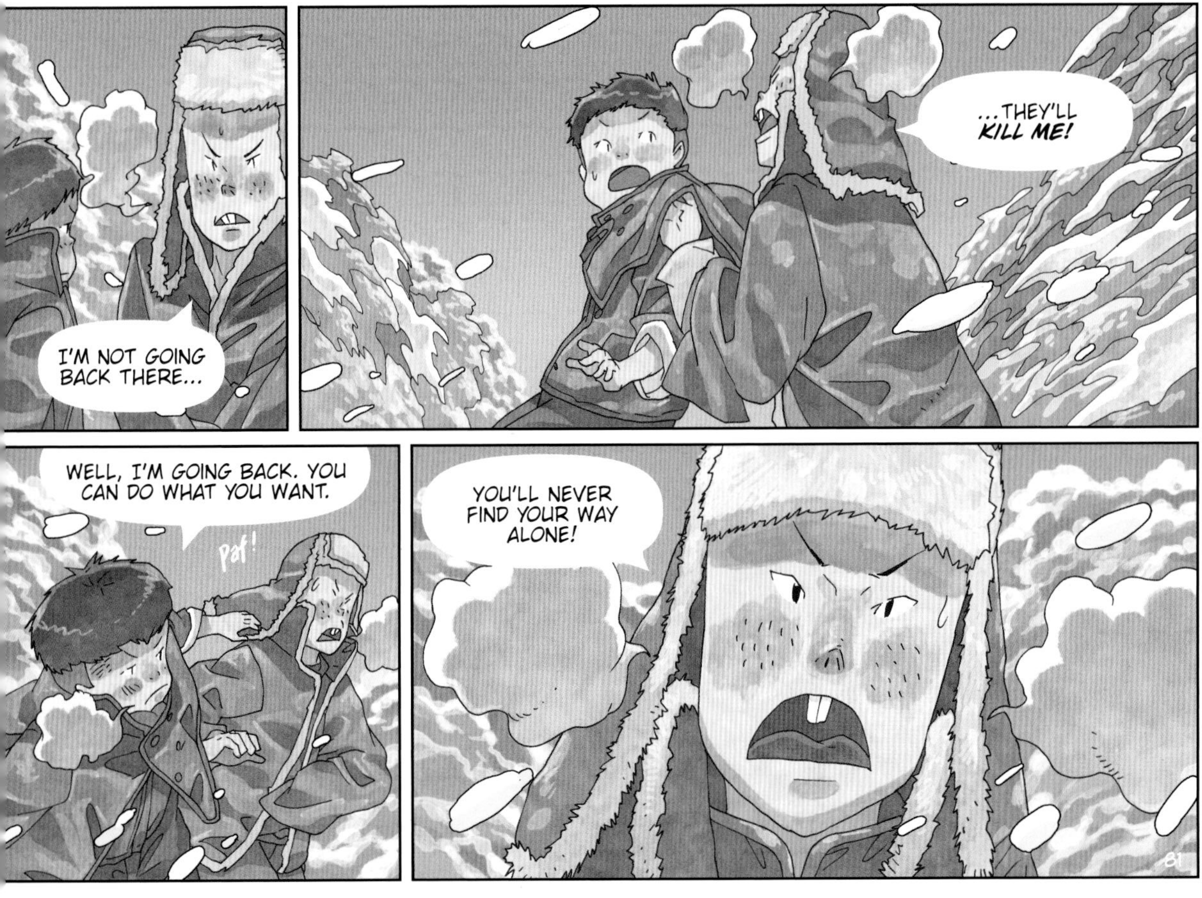
I'M NOT GOING BACK THERE...
...THEY'LL KILL ME!
WELL, I'M GOING BACK. YOU CAN DO WHAT YOU WANT.
Paf!
YOU'LL NEVER FIND YOUR WAY ALONE!

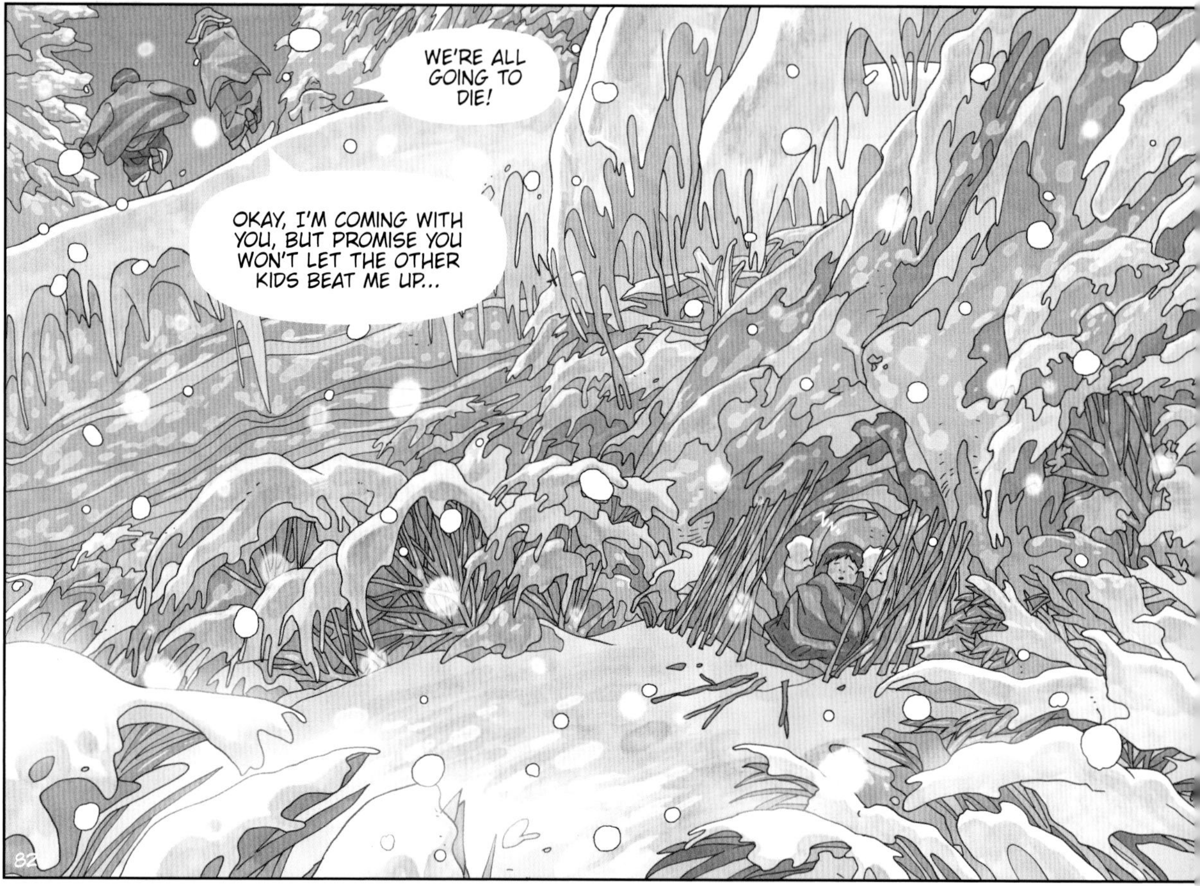
WE'RE ALL GOING TO DIE!
OKAY, I'M COMING WITH YOU, BUT PROMISE YOU WON'T LET THE OTHER KIDS BEAT ME UP...

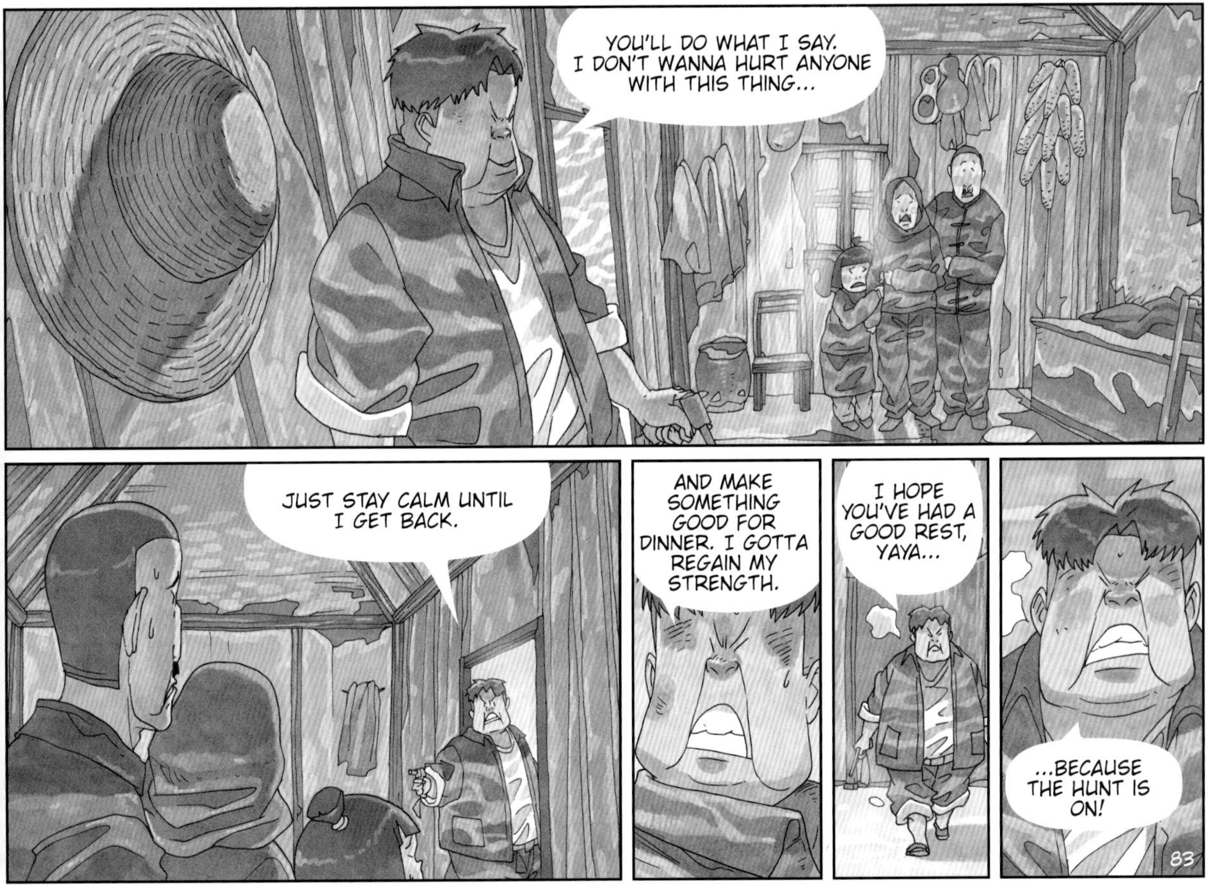
YOU'LL DO WHAT I SAY. I DON'T WANNA HURT ANYONE WITH THIS THING...
JUST STAY CALM UNTIL I GET BACK.
AND MAKE SOMETHING GOOD FOR DINNER. I GOTTA REGAIN MY STRENGTH.
I HOPE YOU'VE HAD A GOOD REST, YAYA...
...BECAUSE THE HUNT IS ON!
83

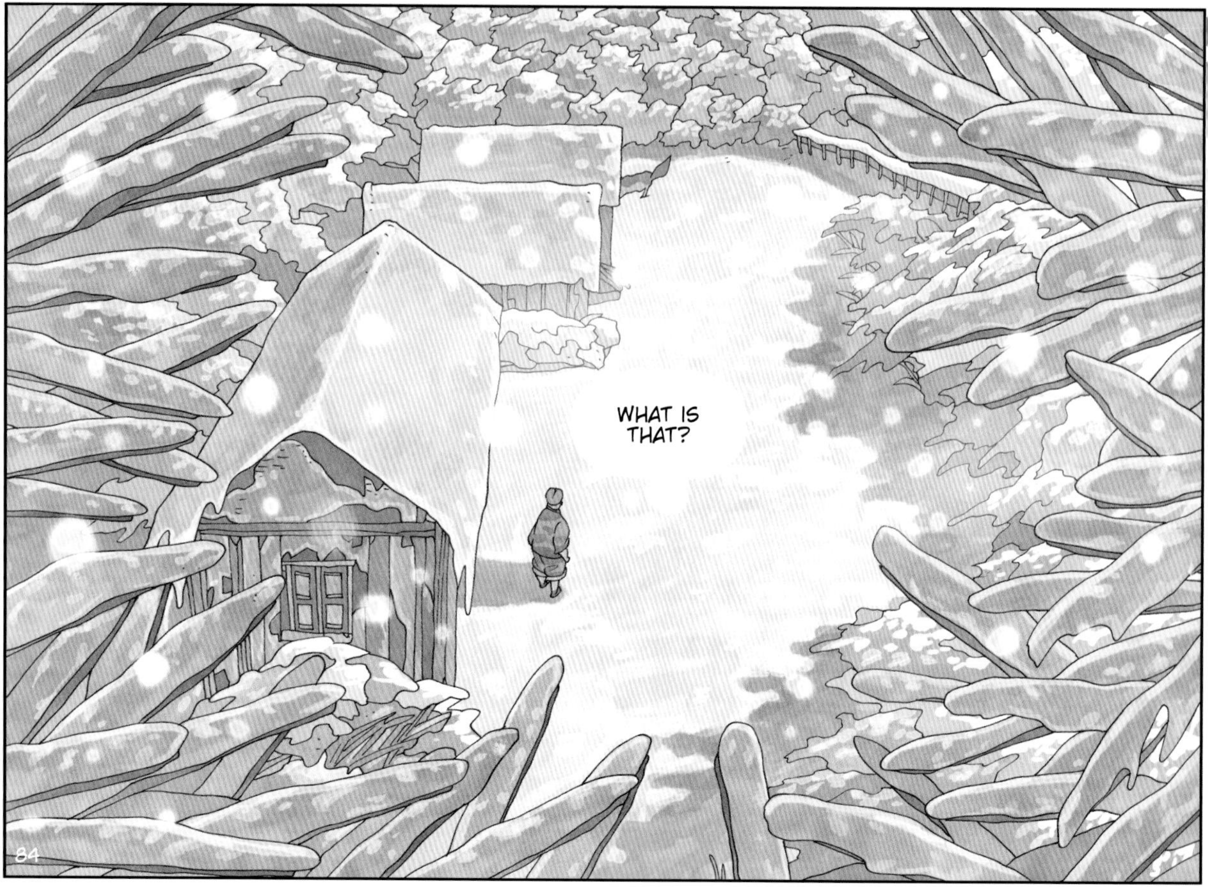
WHAT IS
THAT?

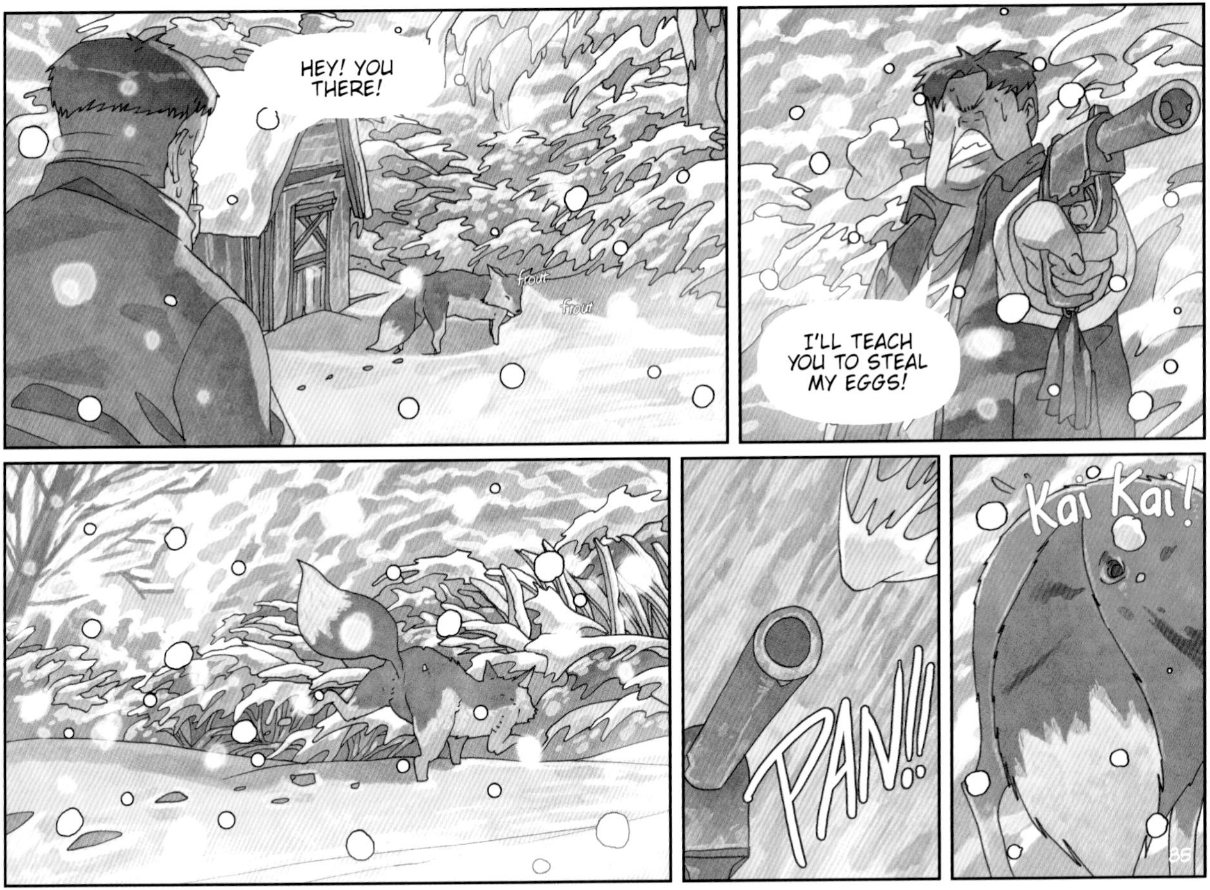
HEY! YOU THERE!
frout
frout
I'LL TEACH YOU TO STEAL MY EGGS!
PAN!!!
Kai Kai!

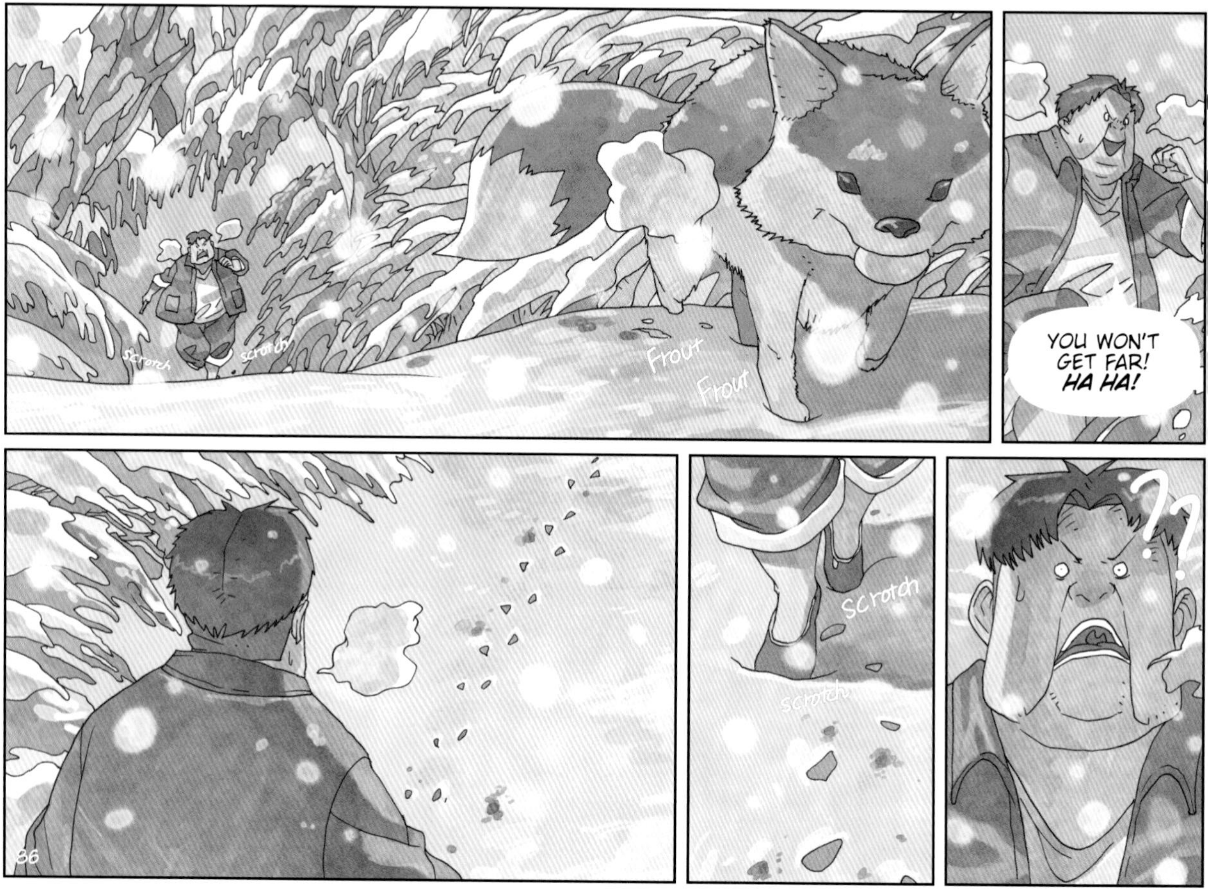

Scrotch
scrotch
Frout
Frout
YOU WON'T GET FAR! HA HA!
Scrotch
scrotch

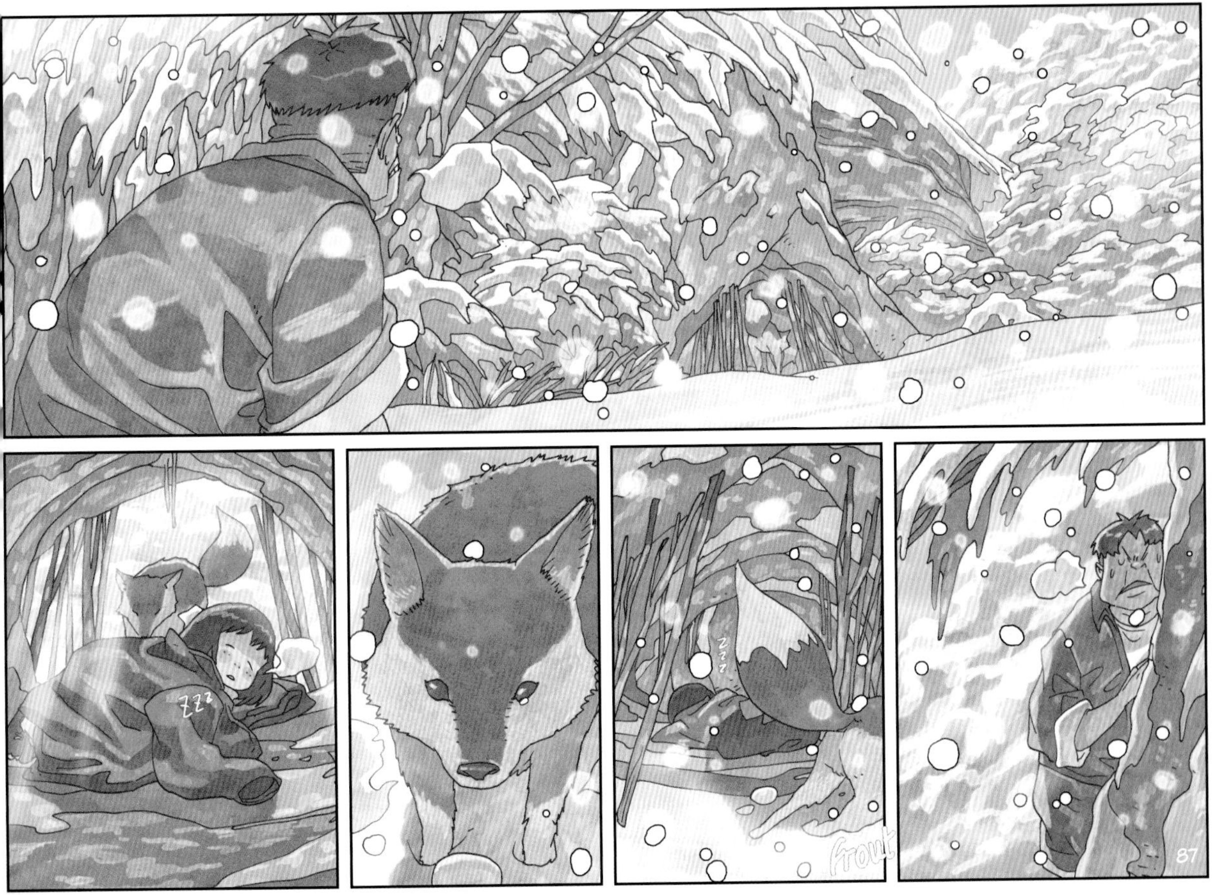
ZZZ
ZZZ
Frout

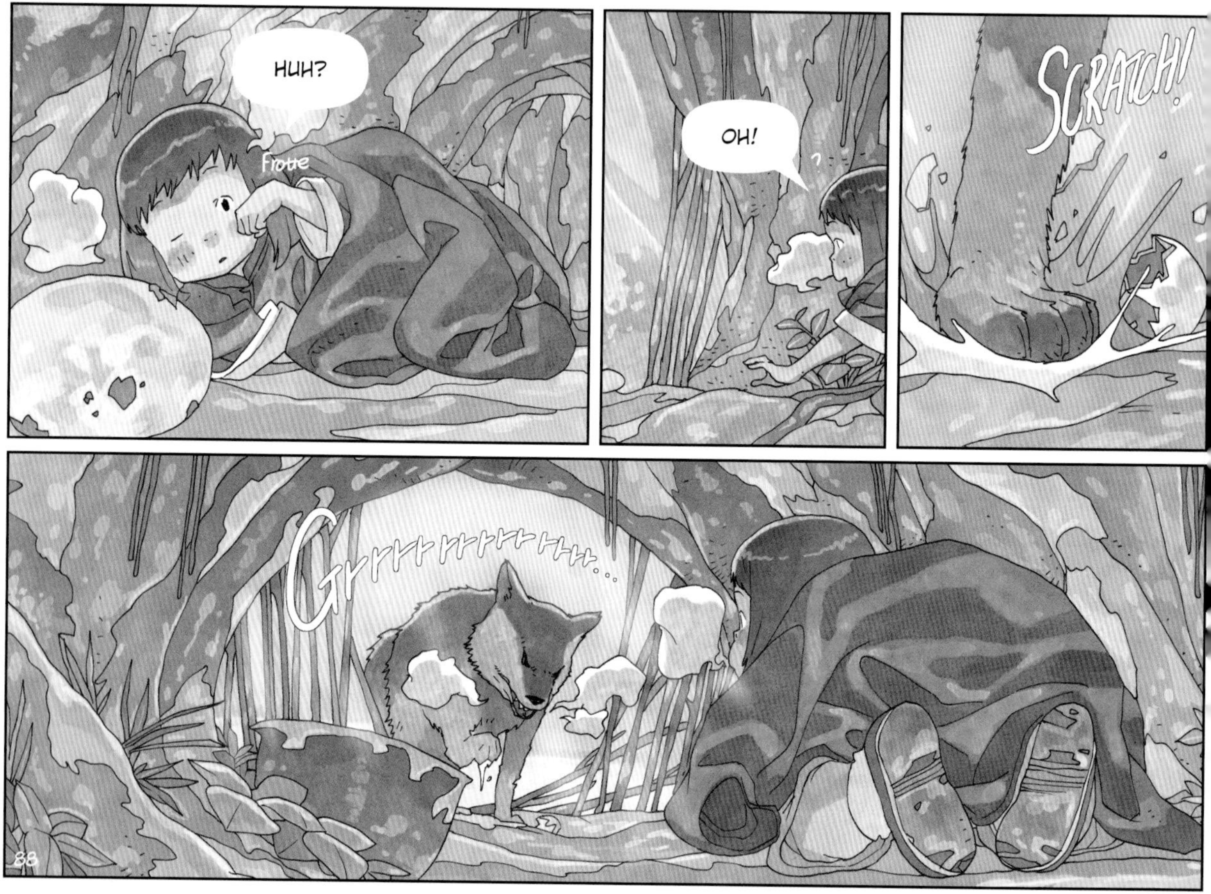
HUH?
Frotte
OH!
SCRATCH!
Grrrrrrrrrrrrr...

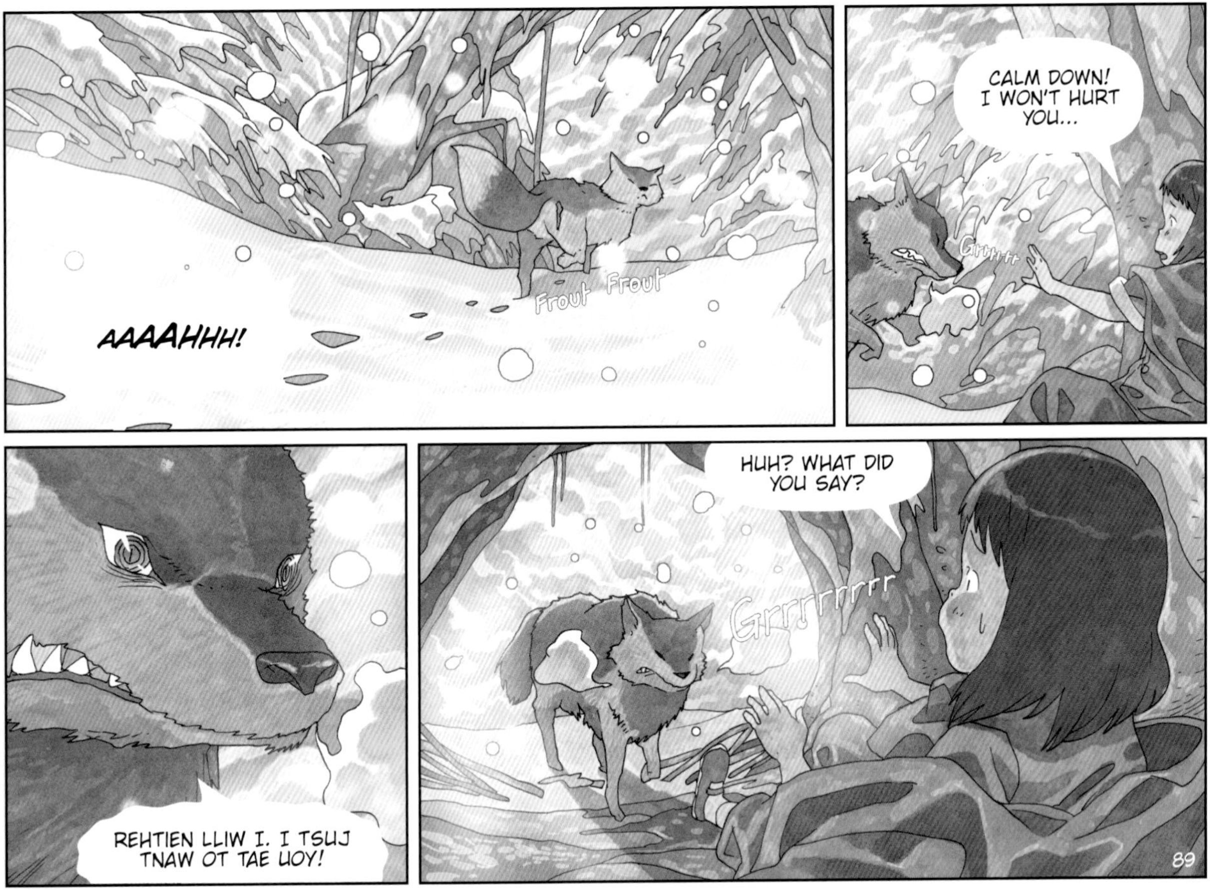
Frout Frout
AAAAHHH!
CALM DOWN! I WON'T HURT YOU...
Grrrrrr
REHTIEN LLIW I. I TSUJ TNAW OT TAE UOY!
HUH? WHAT DID YOU SAY?
Grrrrrrrr

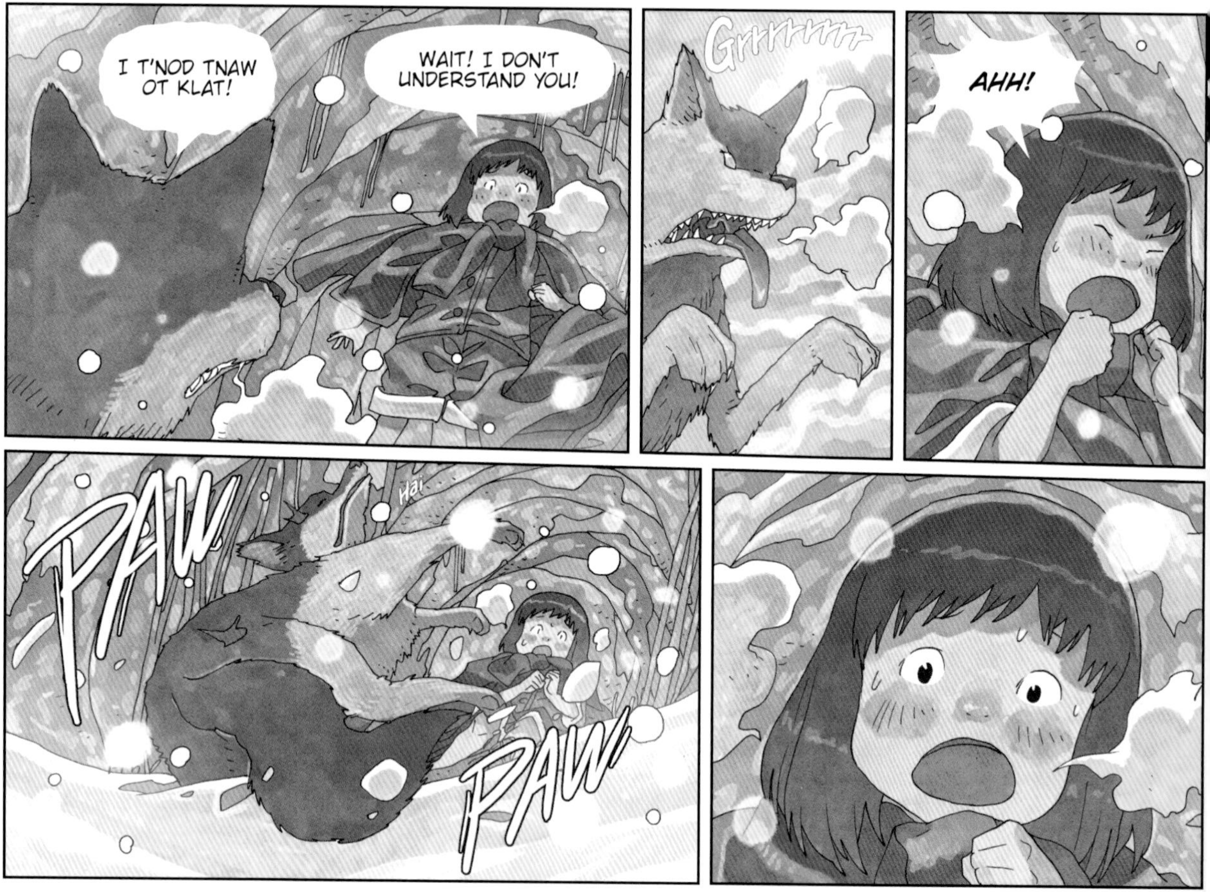
I T'NOD TNAW OT KLAT!
WAIT! I DON'T UNDERSTAND YOU!
Grrrrrrrr
AHH!
PAW
Hai
PAW

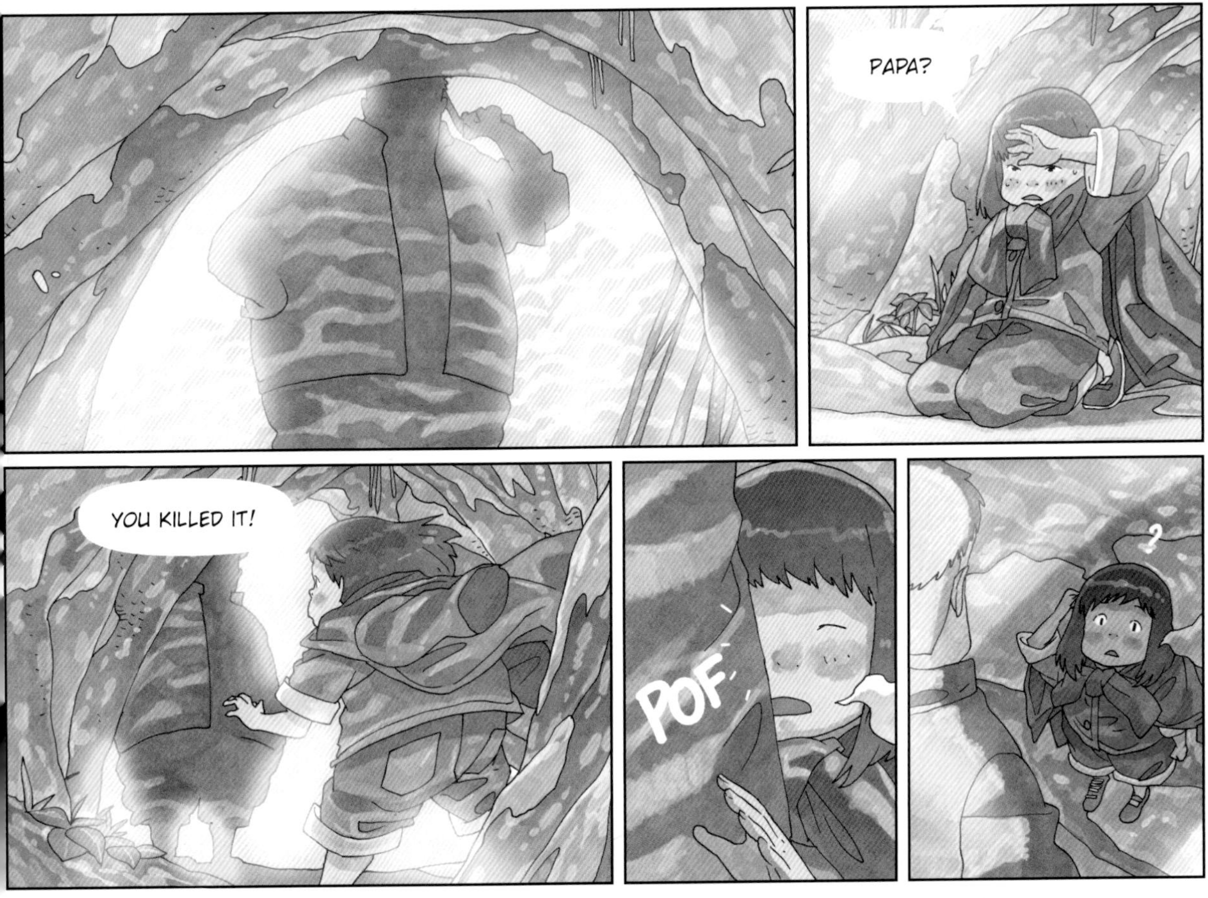
PAPA?
YOU KILLED IT!
POF
?

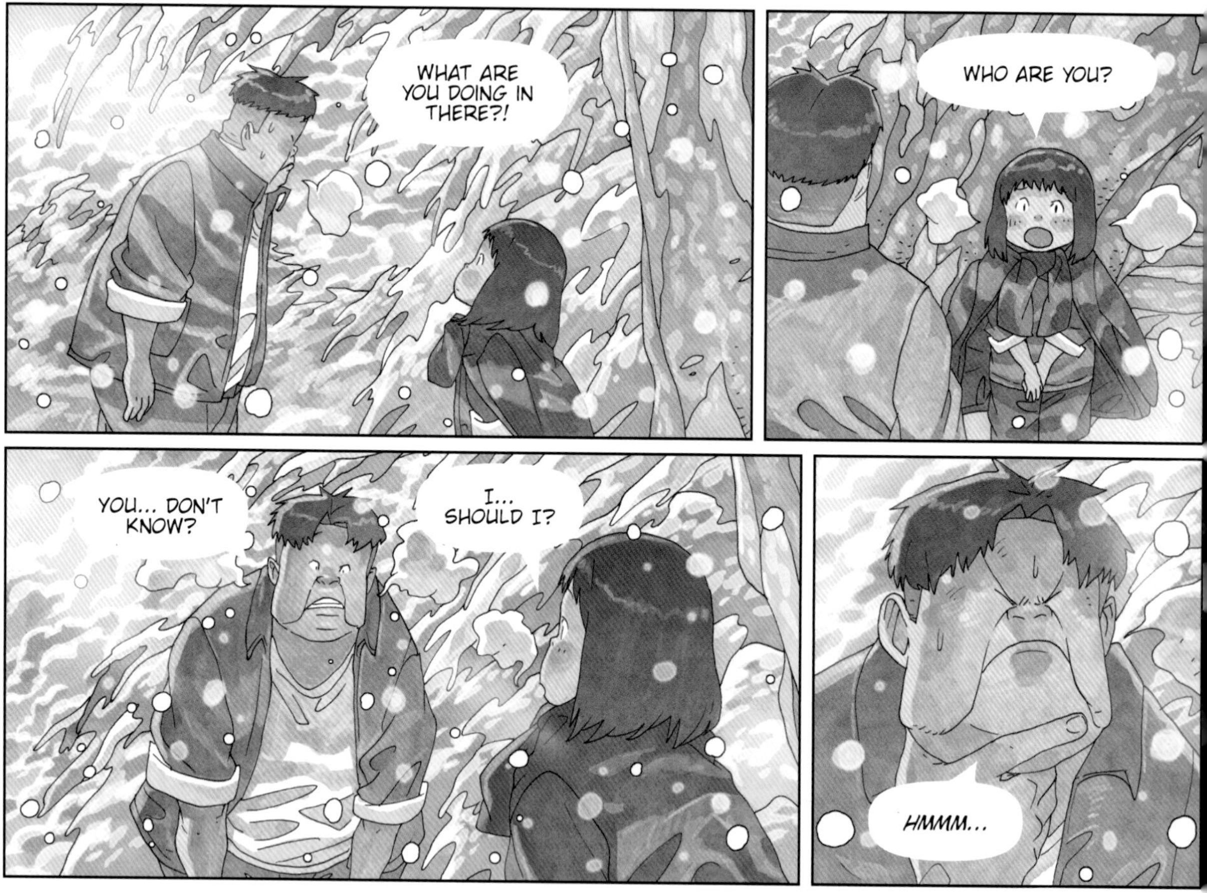
WHAT ARE YOU DOING IN THERE?!
WHO ARE YOU?
YOU... DON'T KNOW?
I... SHOULD I?
HMMM...

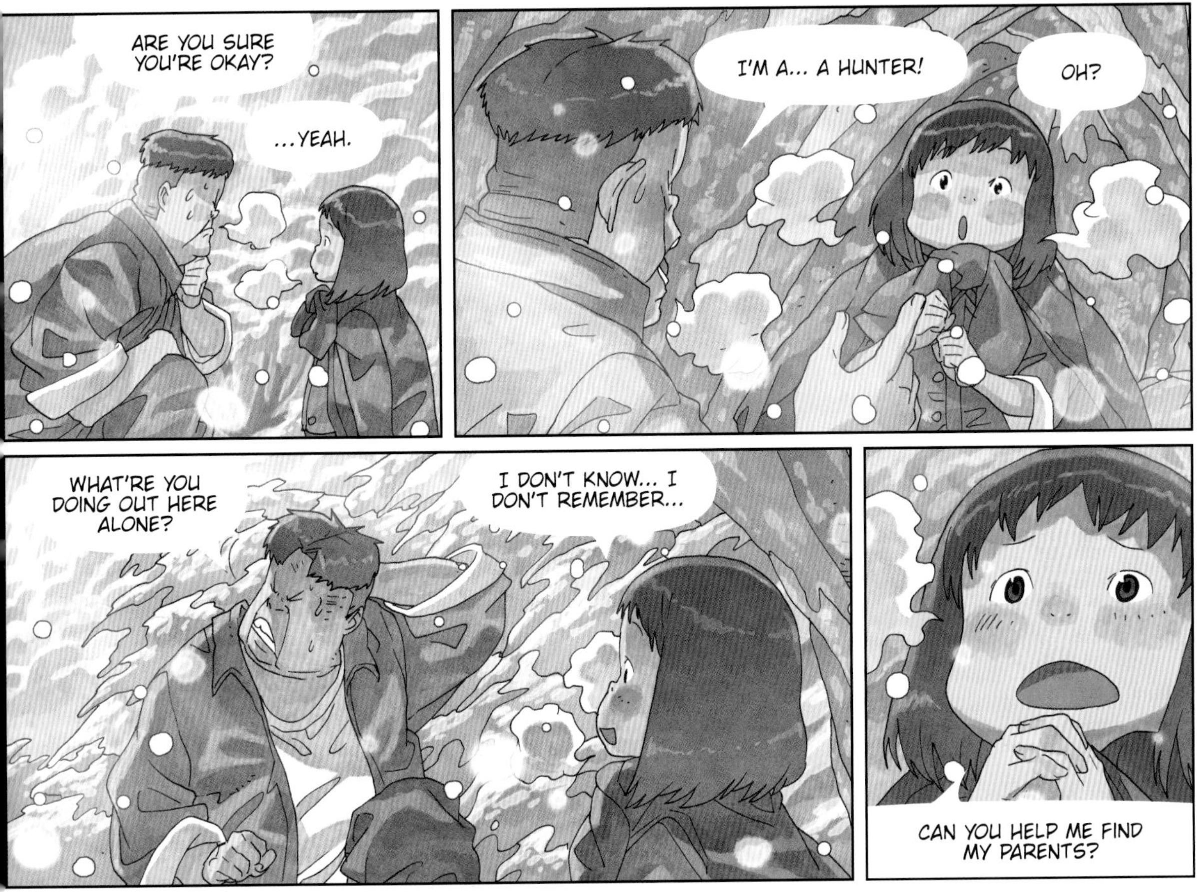
ARE YOU SURE YOU'RE OKAY?
...YEAH.
I'M A... A HUNTER!
OH?
WHAT'RE YOU DOING OUT HERE ALONE?
I DON'T KNOW... I DON'T REMEMBER...
CAN YOU HELP ME FIND MY PARENTS?

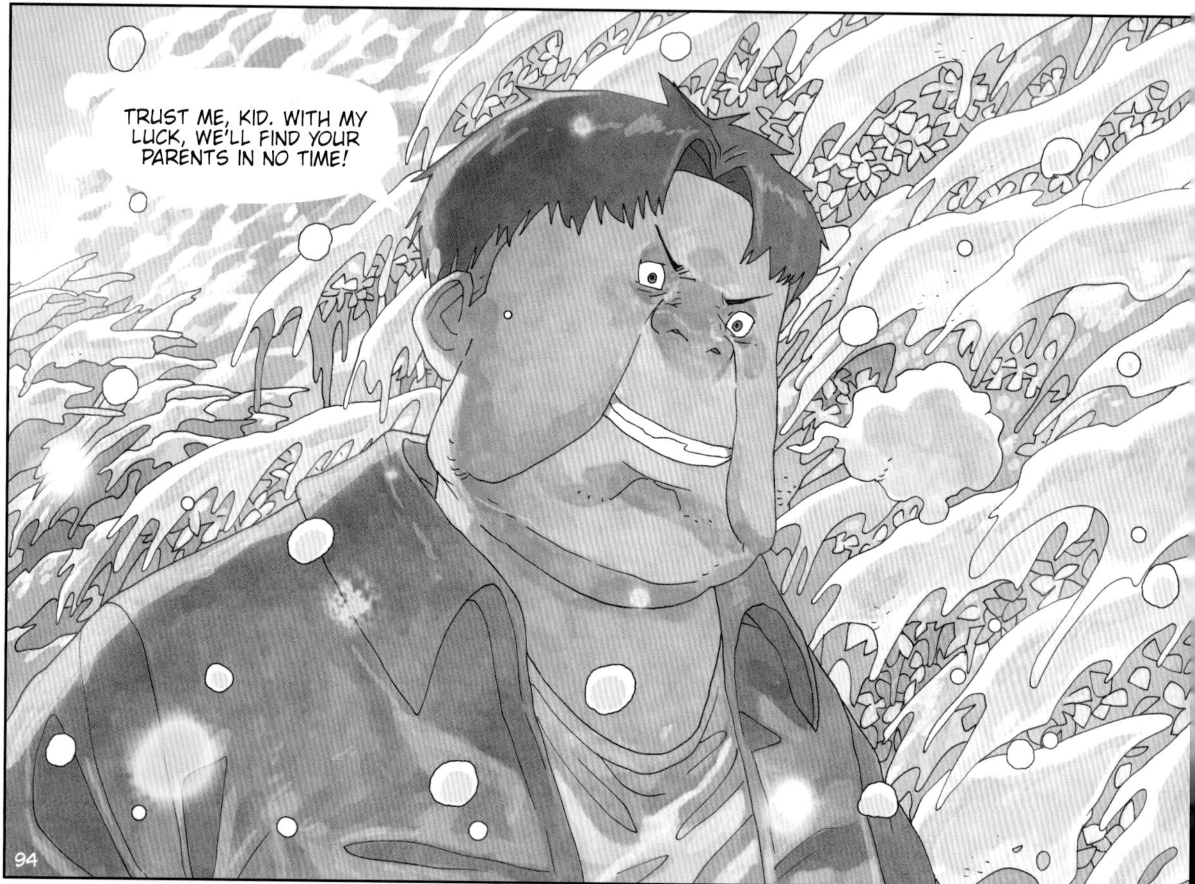
TRUST ME, KID. WITH MY LUCK, WE'LL FIND YOUR PARENTS IN NO TIME!